BETRAYAL

The Haunting Emma series by Lee Nichols

Deception
Betrayal

BETRAYAL

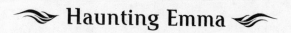 Haunting Emma

Lee Nichols

BLOOMSBURY

NEW YORK BERLIN LONDON SYDNEY

First published in the United States of America in March 2011
by Bloomsbury Books for Young Readers
www.bloomsburyteens.com

For information about permission to reproduce selections from this book, write to
Permissions, Bloomsbury BFYR, 175 Fifth Avenue, New York, New York 10010

Library of Congress Cataloging-in-Publication Data
Nichols, Lee.
Betrayal / by Lee Nichols. — 1st U.S. ed.
p.   cm.
Summary: After learning that she is descended from a legendary ghostkeeper, Emma faces
terrible forces as she tries to dispel Neos, find her family, and discover a way to be with Bennett
without either of them losing their powers.
ISBN 978-1-59990-569-3 (hardcover) • ISBN 978-1-59990-422-1 (paperback)
[1. Ghosts—Fiction.   2. Supernatural—Fiction.   3. Interpersonal relations—
Fiction.   4. Boston (Mass.)—Fiction.]   I. Title.
PZ7.N5412Bet 2011   [Fic]—dc22   2010017350

Book design by Nicole Gastonguay
Typeset by Westchester Book Composition
Printed in the U.S.A. by Quad/Graphics, Fairfield, Pennsylvania
2 4 6 8 10 9 7 5 3 1 (hardcover)
2 4 6 8 10 9 7 5 3 1 (paperback)

All papers used by Bloomsbury Publishing, Inc., are natural, recyclable products
made from wood grown in well-managed forests. The manufacturing processes
conform to the environmental regulations of the country of origin.

Sparks wheeled in the air as the blade cut through the falling light and plunged hilt-deep into the wraith's empty eye socket. The wraith melted to the ground, hollow screams echoing in the evening.

"Tell your master he's next," I said.

Then I pulled my dagger from its eye, broke its neck, and fainted.

I didn't remember the car ride home, except for one odd flash of conversation.

"I've never seen her like that," Natalie said.

"No one's ever seen anyone like that," Simon said, his voice hard.

I woke in my own bed in the middle of the night and gasped in panic. Then I groped around in the dark and found the dagger under the extra pillow on the bed.

My hand closed on the hilt and I fell back to sleep.

1

It's not easy watching a friend get buried, especially when you were responsible for his death.

We're here today to mourn the untimely passing of Coby Jameson Anders. Sixteen years old, honor student, high school quarterback, beloved son and friend.

A week had passed since the murder, and I loitered at the gates of the cemetery, listening to the dean's eulogy while the casket slowly dropped into the ground. Standing at the gates because Coby's best friends—*my* best friends—had banned me from the funeral.

"You're not wanted, Emma," Sara had said.

"Communi consilio," Harry added. Translation: by common consent.

Great. What kind of person gets banned from a funeral? The kind who can't reveal the truth about what happened, because no one would believe her.

His death was a shock to us all. Those who loved him . . .

A ghost killed Coby. Not me. But I was there, and I didn't save him.

Outwardly a happy, well-adjusted, popular young man, Coby kept his true feelings to himself. It's a lesson to us . . .

I shuddered in my peacoat, the November cold penetrating the thin wool, and watched the crowd through the iron gates. Hundreds of mourners stood in a ragged crescent around the grave, Coby's family and friends, teachers from school. They thought he'd killed himself. They hadn't just lost Coby, they'd lost their fondest memories of him, second-guessing his happiness and his easy smile.

Sometimes God's plan seems unjust, unfair. We'll never know why Coby chose to leave us, but hope that he rests easy in the afterlife.

Amid the tears, the priest gave his final blessing, and the mourners tossed dirt on the grave and filed from the cemetery. I fled, my back toward the entrance, unwilling to face the looks of grief and disapproval.

I wandered the village, past the clapboard houses crowded tightly together, down the narrow, winding streets toward the harbor, too cold now for the yachts. I carefully avoided the pond where Coby had died, its surface covered with a thin layer of ice.

I ached to be home in San Francisco, where flowers would still be in bloom and the sun still shone. Here in Massachusetts, the leafless maples loomed overhead, people's lawns had gone all brown, and dead blossoms littered the gardens. As if I needed something else to be depressed about.

I don't know who said from death comes life—probably one of those old, important dead guys—but I eventually circled back to the cemetery, ready to do my part. Ready to breathe a little warmth into this cold world.

As I reached the gates, a flurry of snow suddenly filtered through the gray day, and little white puff balls floated from the sky. I smiled at the clouds, tears filling my eyes, remembering Martha, who'd told me my first snow would be magical.

I caught a snowflake on my tongue, then stepped into the cemetery. Time for more magic. Time to raise the dead.

Here's the thing about ghostkeepers. When we die, we die. There's no coming back like other people: we're cremated or buried and that's the end.

But people like Coby could be summoned. Or at least, their ghosts could.

I surveyed the empty cemetery, snow dusting the granite tombstones, then wove through the monuments to stand at Coby's grave. I bowed my head and looked at the coffin, scattered with dirt and flowers, but didn't toss in my own handful of dirt, because to me he'd soon no longer be dead. I licked my lips, suddenly nervous. What if he hated me? What if he wasn't the same? Or worse, what if he didn't want to come back?

I took a deep breath. Only one way to find out.

I closed my eyes and felt the chill air go still around

me. I'd never done this before, summoned a ghost who wasn't already lingering in the Beyond. I knew I could, though—despite being new to ghostkeeping, I was powerful. Almost too powerful. Maybe if I hadn't been, Neos would've ignored me, and Coby would still be alive.

Well, I couldn't change the past, but I could alter Coby's future. I raised my face to the sky, letting the snowflakes tickle my cheeks, feeling the energy of the Beyond. It got easier all the time to identify the supernatural tug of ghosts. Of course, standing in the middle of a cemetery probably helped.

My eyes shut, I heard the pounding of my heart and felt the blood rushing through my veins, as my summoning energy expanded beyond my body. Tendrils of power flowered through the cemetery until I sensed Coby's slumbering spirit curled nearby, as though waiting for me. I summoned him, tugging him gently toward our world. His spirit seemed to recognize mine and came willingly.

With a sudden rush, I knew that I'd succeeded. I opened my eyes, waiting for his soft arrival. Instead, when Coby's ghost slipped into our world, a blinding burst of spectral lightning flashed. I jumped backward in surprise, and the wet snow combined with mud at the edge of the pit gave way.

I yelped as I fell into the grave.

"Crap!" I sprawled atop Coby's casket on my butt. A noise I didn't recognize escaped my throat—half revulsion and half amusement. The scent of freshly dug earth surrounded me. I covered my mouth with my hand, then noticed my palm was covered in grave muck. "Bleh!"

I stood—yes, still on top of Coby's casket—and prayed his parents didn't return. This was bad. This was toss-Emma-back-into-the-mental-hospital bad.

I spun, looking for a way out, and discovered Coby beside me, still in the suit he'd worn for Homecoming. Except now he was slightly transparent and his suit didn't fit quite so well—and it didn't seem possible, but he was even better looking.

Welcome back, I said to him.

Emma! You're all dirty.

Yeah. I, um, slipped.

He stepped forward with a crooked grin to wipe my face. *I knew I should've taken hand wipes to Homecoming.*

Wait, I said. *You can't touch me.*

The grin turned to a smile. *Is this some kind of purity-ring thing?*

Actually, it was a ghosts-burn-ghostkeepers thing.

No, I said. *I, um . . . What's the last thing you remember?*

He focused into the distance. *Wait, yeah, what happened? I drove to your house and you looked so hot in that dress and we stepped outside and . . .* He didn't quite pale, already being a ghost and all. *It was like a bad dream.*

It wasn't a dream, Coby.

I didn't know where to start, what to tell him first. Did he remember Neos? Did he know his death was all my fault?

He faded until I saw the dirt wall clearly behind him,

and his face grew haggard and grim with memory. I watched his faint eyes as he recalled everything: Neos possessing his body, then trying to drown me in the pond, my turning into a ghost and battling Neos before fleeing and abandoning him.

Who are you? he finally asked.

I'm Emma. I'm still Emma.

I mean what *are you?*

I'm a ghostkeeper. I see and compel and communicate with ghosts. I dispel them and . . .

And what?

I summon them.

Oh God, he said. *Oh God. I'm a ghost!*

He faded, and I called out, "Coby! Coby, come back! I'm sorry—please, I'm so sorry!"

The wind whispered through the branches of faraway trees as he disappeared completely. Leaving me alone with my aching need to make things right with him.

You're sorry? he said, materializing behind me.

When I turned, his face looked harder with knowledge and determination, and I flinched. He'd vanished into the Beyond, where a ghost had once explained to me that time wasn't the same. It moved slower there, giving Coby a chance to think.

Everything's changed, he said, his voice rough.

I know. How you can ever forgive—

Forgive you? I'm dead because of you. And you still couldn't leave me alone.

He stepped nearer, and his grave seemed to grow

smaller, the walls tightening around me. A wave of nausea rose from my stomach at the earthy smell and the knowledge that I was standing on top of Coby's dead body—and at the look in his eyes, intent and furious. He was right—everything *had* changed—especially him.

He took another step and raised his hand to hover at the bare skin of my cheek. *I'll burn you if I touch you, won't I?*

Coby, please. Please don't, I said, as I met his unearthly gaze. I couldn't bear his transformation, or how much it reminded me of when Neos possessed him. This wasn't the Coby I remembered. That boy never would've wanted to harm me, even if I deserved it.

Give me one reason why, Emma, he said. *One reason you shouldn't have to share my pain.*

And that's just it. I couldn't. So I stepped into him, pressing his fingers to my face.

Pain flared on my cheek for an instant before Coby pulled back.

What are you doing? he asked. *Haven't you heard of dramatic effect? I don't want to hurt you.*

You don't? I wouldn't blame you if you did.

No, I just— He frowned at his semitransparent hand. *I can't believe I'm really dead. Forget about graduation. Forget about prom, forget about college. I'll never play football, I'll never hear music or—*

You'll hear music, Coby. I'll play whatever you want.

His sad smile broke my heart. *What am I supposed to do now?*

I don't know. Go see your parents? Sara and Harry miss you. I don't know what your life will be like—

He shot me a look. *My what?*

Okay, wrong word. Your existence?

A short nod.

I don't know what it's going to be like being a ghost. I'm not even sure what it's like to be a ghostkeeper. Sometimes I wish there were a manual. But I promise you two things. I'll always be here for you. And I'm going to find Neos—I'm going to kill him for what he did to you.

He nodded slowly, then met my gaze. *I'll help you do it.*

Oh! I smiled in relief that he didn't hate me. *I was just hoping you'd still talk to me.*

It's not like I've got so many other people to talk to. And you need all the help you can get.

Nah, I said, trying to reassure him. *I've got everything under control.*

Other than being trapped in my grave? Too bad you're not a ghost—if you were, you could do this. He shot me a crooked grin, like the old Coby, and vanished.

He had a point.

Okay, so you've fallen into a grave. Your ghost friend abandons you, you're cold and wet and wishing you'd worked more on your biceps. How do you get yourself out?

I wasn't about to use the original Emma's ring to turn into a ghost. Not only because this was so ridiculous, but because I didn't know if there were any side effects, like that ring in Tolkien. All I needed was to start gibbering about *my preciousssss.*

Instead, I hurled myself at the muddy wall and clawed upward until I reached the top of the open grave and grabbed a handful of grass. My boots skidded and slipped as I got another grassy handhold and dragged myself out.

I lay on the ground, panting and aching and wondering how I'd ever get the mud out of the only coat I owned. The snow drifted down and the cold soaked into my sore fingers.

And a pair of worn lace-up boots appeared beside my head. Perfect. The groundskeeper. Probably about to call the police.

"What happened?" he asked.

I knew that voice, like I knew the taste of a hot red-eye chai on a cold morning. I looked up at him, feeling a glow of warmth despite the weather. Bennett. He wore a navy wool coat over a gray sweater and slim jeans, looking casual and gorgeous.

"Thank God it's you," I said.

He took my hand—very briefly—and helped me to my feet. "I thought I'd find you here. Only not looking quite so muddy." He glanced into the grave. "Did you . . . ?"

"I fell, okay?"

"Then clawed your way out like a bad zombie movie?"

I brushed dirt from my peacoat. "Could've happened to anyone."

He chuckled. "Yeah, your first real summoning. The flash surprises everyone."

"You might've warned me."

"I would have, if I'd known you were coming so soon," he said. "He's not even buried yet."

"Tell me something I don't know."

He gestured to the side of his head. "You've got a little something . . ."

I pulled a dead beetle from my hair. "Gah."

He bit his lip, trying not to laugh.

"It's all right." I sighed. "I'd laugh, too, if I weren't freezing and slug-ridden. And do I smell?"

"Maybe a little," he admitted. "C'mon, I'll take you home."

He moved to put his arm around me, which was brave considering I stank like Swamp Thing. "I'm okay," I said, stepping away from him.

Bennett reluctantly let his arm drop, then stuck both hands in the pockets of his coat. "How did it go?"

I shrugged. "He's back."

"Is he different?"

"A little." We walked toward the gates of the cemetery. "His clothes don't fit right, and I don't know . . . he's sadder and sharper. And even better looking."

Bennett grunted.

"Not that I care," I said. "I mean, I do care. I'm glad he's back. But I don't care that he's gorgeous. That's not the only reason I wanted him back. I mean, that's not why I summoned him at all. Why am I even talking about this?"

Bennett nudged me with his elbow. "You're nervous. It's a big deal, summoning a ghost from his grave."

"Plus, he's the only one I knew when he was alive."

"You're not still blaming yourself for his death, are you?"

I huddled silently in my muddy coat and followed Bennett toward his ancient Land Rover. I climbed into the left side, because the car had come over from England and the wheel was on the right.

"It *was* my fault," I finally said. "Both their deaths were."

I'd not only lost Coby, but Martha, who'd been Bennett's nanny growing up. I was amazed he was still talking to me.

"Emma, Neos killed them. Not you."

"If he hadn't been after me—"

"Is it also your fault Neos murdered Olivia?"

I flinched. "Your sister died three blocks from my house."

Bennett pulled away from the curb, and I sat there miserably, holding my cold fingers to the heating vents. Had he not made that connection between me and Olivia's death?

"Say something," I said.

He glanced at me, then forced his eyes back to the road. "You're right about one thing—if Neos hadn't been after you, Coby and Martha would still be alive. But you didn't pull the trigger, Emma; that's like blaming a deer for a hunting accident. Neos didn't kill my sister because of you. And what's the alternative? That you're dead and they're not?"

He placed his hand on the seat beside me but didn't quite touch me. He wore a thick silver band on one finger, and I traced it with my fingertip, carefully not touching his skin, wondering if his hands were always that warm.

"I'm sorry they're dead," he said. "But I'm glad you're alive."

He turned into the museum gates and drove down the maple-lined drive toward his family home, a Federal-period house that during the summer was a museum open to the public. I'd been staying there with Bennett and our friend Natalie, also a ghostkeeper, since Coby's death. We'd basically shut out the rest of the world after losing so much to Neos.

"We need to find him," I said.

"Yeah," Bennett agreed. "Find him and dispel him."

He parked, and I watched him walk around to my side, liking everything about him. His voice, the way he moved, the way he dressed in boho-preppy clothing that you only ever saw on New England college kids. But mostly I loved who he was, that he was loyal and protective. He even opened my door—such a gentleman.

"It's going to be okay, Emma. We're going to stop him. Together."

Bennett had once told me that when Neos was gone,

he'd be with me, even if that meant losing his ghostkeeping abilities. I followed him into the house, wanting to touch him, to press myself against him—but how do you ask someone to make that kind of sacrifice? Unlike me, Bennett had been raised as a ghostkeeper; it was all he'd ever known.

Could I really ask him to give that up? Would he be the same guy I fell for without it?

2

I didn't think I'd ever tire of walking into the museum. The French blue, sea green, and pale yellow palette of the walls and furnishings always comforted me, along with the hearty scent that wafted in from the kitchen.

Bennett leafed through the mail, then asked if I'd be ready to leave in a couple of hours. "I know the timing's not great, so soon after the funeral, but they're expecting us."

"They" were the Knell, the covert society that ruled the ghostkeeping world. Actually, I wasn't exactly sure what they did. Sometimes they sounded like the secret police, other times like a crazy cult. Bennett had made an appointment for us to meet them at their headquarters in Manhattan.

"They're really going to help us?"

He nodded. "This is what they do. They've been investigating Neos, and Yoshiro knows more about this stuff than anyone."

"Who's Yoshiro?"

"The leader of the Knell. Not the friendliest guy in the world, but he'll know exactly how to beat Neos."

I brushed at the mud on my coat, thinking about the Knell. "Is it like CONTROL in that *Get Smart* movie?"

"No," Bennett said. "Although they do have the Cone of Silence."

My eyes lit up. "Really?"

"Yeah, and you enter the building through—"

"A *telephone booth*?"

"Porta-potty."

"Oh, ha-ha."

He smiled. "Are you going to be ready to hit the train at three?"

"As long as I can eat first," I said, starting upstairs to pack. "Though I'd be faster if you had a shoe phone."

He turned back to the mail. "I'll see what I can do."

I smiled, but my stomach soured. I didn't want to go. The Knell and I didn't exactly have a cordial relationship. Admittedly, the only members I knew were Bennett and Natalie, who were also my only friends at the moment. But back in San Francisco, the Knell had ordered Natalie to get me into trouble with the cops, and Bennett to play my savior. It'd taken a while to forgive them, with Martha helping me work through the deception. I hadn't quite forgiven the Knell yet.

On the other hand, the Knell was my best chance—maybe my only chance—to find both Neos and my missing family.

Upstairs, I found Nicholas in the hallway, listening at
Natalie's door. Even while lurking, his youth made him
seem innocent. From the look of him, he'd died sometime
during the Dickensian era. "Food, Glorious Food" could
spring from his lips at any moment.

What are you doing? I asked.

She won't stop crying. Even after I made her a fire.

Nicholas laid the fires and polished the silver and did
whatever other tasks Anatole and Celeste deemed below
their dignity. Gotta love a household staff of ghosts.

I'll take care of her, I said. *Go find something to eat, will ya?*

I wish, he mumbled, before fading out.

Oh yeah, he couldn't eat. *Sorry,* I called after him, then
knocked on Natalie's door. "It's me."

She cried harder.

I went in and found her curled in a fetal position on
the bed, not bothering to look up. The room was a mirror
image of my own, with antique furnishings and a minuscule fireplace, but hers was in shades of yellow, while
mine was blue green. I plopped down next to her and
started rubbing circles on her back.

She took a shuddering breath. "I like ghosts," she said, in
a small voice. "I've never been afraid of them, you know?"
She turned her face toward me and I grabbed a box of tissues from the bureau to wipe her tears.

"Blow," I said.

She rolled her eyes. "Thanks, Mom," she said, lifting
tissues from the box.

"Well, right now . . ." I left the rest unspoken. We

were both missing our moms, and with Martha gone, we kind of had to fill in for each other. I brushed her hair behind her ears and silently encouraged her to tell me what brought this on.

"It was just seeing his casket go into the grave. I knew you were going to summon him later, but he won't be the same, will he?"

"Not quite," I said, looking at the gray light filtering through the window. "He's sad. I don't remember his ever being sad."

"And then—this is totally selfish—but I couldn't help thinking about me. All those people there. If I died, who'd even come to the funeral? Do you think my parents would care?"

"I'm sure they—"

She blew her nose. "I don't even have a family anymore. I chose seeing ghosts over my parents. And now I drift from place to place, wherever the Knell sends me. What kind of life is that?"

"I don't know."

"A crappy one."

"But, Natalie, look at you. You're the queen of coping. You're pretty and fun and you make friends everywhere you go."

"I'm in eleventh grade and this is my fifth high school." She sniffled. "You know the Knell is paying for Thatcher?"

Thatcher Academy was the private school we both attended, with uniforms and fencing classes and old money. I'd wondered who was footing the bill for both of us, but had been too preoccupied by the fact that I could control ghosts to ask about it.

"They already told me they'll pay for college," she said.

"That's a good thing, right?"

She grimaced. "They saved my life." She'd been in a bad situation, before Bennett stepped in and rescued her. "But when am I going to stop owing them? I don't think they'd care if I died."

"Natalie, stop. You're not going to die. And *I'd* care."

"You would?"

I took her hand. "Of course. And so would Bennett. We're your family now."

She gave me a watery smile. "We do bicker like sisters."

"Exactly!"

I hugged her and she said, "Um, now that we're sisters, I feel I can say that you need to do something about that smell."

"I fell into Coby's grave."

She started laughing, like I'd hoped she would. Her mood lightened and, with that crisis averted, I told her I had to pack for the appointment with the Knell.

I was at the door when she said, "Emma, don't let them split us up."

"Why would they?"

"They don't like us to get too close. But they'll listen to you."

I frowned. We *were* like family, and the Knell had played manipulative games to get us together. I hated the idea that they might try to separate us. And what did that mean for me and Bennett? Did the Knell know how close we were getting? Were they going to send Bennett away? My heart constricted at the thought.

"I won't let them," I promised, though I wasn't sure how I'd stop them.

But it was enough for Natalie. She nodded, looking relieved.

I crossed the hall to the bathroom and set the shower to blistering. I stepped in and scrubbed my hair and skin, trying to scrape away the feelings along with the dirt: all the anxiety, pain, and fear from the last week. It didn't work, but at least I no longer stank.

My bedroom was down the hall, across from an oil painting of one of Bennett's stuffier-looking ancestors. Inside, I found my suitcase open on the bed where Celeste—the resident ghost maid—had undoubtedly left it. She knew I didn't like her packing for me, but she always wanted to help. I put on black jeans and a gray wool sweater, then rifled through my clothes. After a minute's thought, I packed everything else I owned that was black. In New York, I wanted to blend in.

I was zipping my suitcase when my stomach rumbled. I'd skipped breakfast that morning, nervous about summoning Coby, and was suddenly starving. I went downstairs to the kitchen for a few bites of whatever was filling the house with a delicious smell.

I found Anatole pulling popovers from the oven. Before he died, Anatole had been resident chef to one of Bennett's ancestors, and his spirit had lingered. It was odd how quickly you could get used to a French ghost serving your meals. *Yum. Can I have one now?*

Oui. I made them for you. He slathered one with butter and handed it to me on a blue and white china plate.

Fameux, I told him.

I'd been looking up French words on the Internet to please him. Hopefully *excellent* had the same connotation in French as in English, and I hadn't just said *excellent . . . in bed*, or something. There was no telling with the French. He and Celeste, who was sitting in the breakfast nook, appeared unimpressed, so I guessed it was okay.

What are you up to? I asked, sitting down beside her. It was unlike Celeste not to be occupied with some household task. Unless she was telling Nicholas to do it.

Waiting for you, she said. She was young and pretty, as ghosts went, and wore a gray dress and white apron. I wondered if she ever got tired of that outfit and wished for a day off.

I finished my packing. I bit into the popover, which was like eating a buttered cloud.

Oui, but you are off to ze big city— She gestured to an assortment of beauty products on the table. *I do your hair and makeup.*

Oh. The last time Celeste gave me a makeover, I ended up strapped to a ducking chair and almost drowned. *I don't know if I need . . .*

I will be quick as a quicky quick, she said. Talk about lost in translation.

I don't think that's an expression.

She paid no attention as she drifted behind me and worked product into my hair without touching my scalp.

I finished my popover and brushed crumbs from my chest as she applied blush and mascara. I wiped my mouth with the linen napkin Anatole handed me, then puckered for her to apply lipstick. She fluttered around me for another few minutes, then said, *Fini*, and handed me a mirror.

I looked exactly like myself, only prettier. *I don't know how you do that.*

She'd even made my hair look longer. I'd been trying to grow it, despite remembering with a shiver that Bennett had told me he liked it short. You had to like a guy who wasn't looking for a Barbie doll.

Celeste smiled a secret smile, then told me to be careful in New York.

Oui, chéri, Anatole said, leaning against the table. *You cannot trust those people.*

Which people?

He shrugged meaningfully, but before I could press him, Bennett stepped into the kitchen.

He eyed the three of us at the breakfast nook, and Anatole leaped to serve him a popover while Celeste tidied the makeup away. Bennett frightened them a little, because he couldn't communicate with them, only see them—and dispel them, if he wanted. Which he wouldn't.

I frowned. At least, I thought he wouldn't. Last week I'd finally heard from my mother. She'd left me a photo of Bennett in the mailbox with the cryptic message: *Don't trust him*.

Thank you, Mom, for that detailed letter after you've been missing for two months. So glad to hear that you and Dad are having a marvelous time, wherever you are. Oh, and thanks for keeping the fact that I'm a ghostkeeper a secret all those years. You'll shortly be receiving your nomination for Best Parenting award in the mail. Oh, wait, I don't have your address.

Anyway, I'd crumpled the photo before Bennett saw it, but I still worried about it. Anatole's comment made me wonder if I was supposed to mistrust Bennett because he worked for the Knell. Is that what my parents meant? Or did they know something about Bennett that, as usual, they weren't telling me? And did I even care what they thought?

Bennett downed the popover in three bites, then pressed his hands together in a praying motion and bowed to Anatole, which I thought was nice.

He turned to me. "You ready to go?"

"Yeah," I said, then remembered: "Oh no, my coat." Still covered in grave muck.

It iz cleaned and in ze front hall, Celeste said.

I couldn't hug her without suffering from ghostly frostbite, so I blew a kiss and followed Bennett to the front door.

Watching him carry my suitcase to the car, I couldn't help but remember that the last time we'd gone on a trip together, I'd ended up three thousand miles from home, seeing ghosts, and battling wraiths. I hoped this journey wasn't quite so life changing.

It was a thirty-minute trip to the train station in Boston. Enough time for me to simply enjoy riding around in a car with my boyfriend. I could get used to this.

Ten minutes out of Echo Point, we passed a little shack with a giant, hand-painted ice cream cone bolted to its side. "They make the best ice cream," Bennett said.

The window was shuttered, and it looked as though they hadn't served ice cream for months. "If it's so good, how come they went out of business?"

"They're just closed for the season. Come Memorial Day, I promise I'll take you there."

I tried not to get too excited at the idea of a future together. "Nothing 'closes for the season' in San Francisco. There's only foggy and less foggy. People eat ice cream in both conditions."

"The weather is awesome here in the summer." Bennett glanced at me. "Do you like to sail?"

"Um . . ." I'd actually never been on any boat other than a ferry, but picturing me and Bennett out on a little sailboat in Echo Point harbor was about as romantic as I could dream. "Yeah. I like it a lot."

He smiled. "Good. Because we have a boat. And you and I are on it all summer."

We passed a stretch of ocean on the left. I gazed out at it, longing for summer. Crystal blue water and warm air caressing my skin. Or maybe by then it would be Bennett caressing me. "Will we ever have to come back to shore?"

"Not if we don't want to." He gazed at me hungrily and I tried not to blush.

His look gave me goose bumps and I crossed my arms to keep from shivering. It all seemed so impossible, but a girl could dream. "Sounds like heaven."

We left the Land Rover in long-term parking at the station and caught the bullet train to New York. We sat in plush first-class seats, courtesy of Bennett's family money, and a waiter brought snacks and drinks. They didn't have chai, so I settled for an English Breakfast tea with milk in a cute little plastic teacup, and watched the scenery as we glided down the track.

It was painful, sitting so close to Bennett. He was wearing a navy linen button-down that made his eyes seem almost too blue. I found it hard to focus on what he was saying when I looked straight into them. The problem was, I really wanted to brush his dark bangs out of his eyes, and kiss his perfect lips, and run my hands over his chest, and . . . I gulped my tea.

I couldn't do any of that, because if Bennett and I stayed together, kept touching and kissing and doing everything else we wanted to do, we'd risk our ghost-keeper powers. So I fiddled with my empty teacup and stared out the window, afraid that if I talked to him we'd have more conversations like the one in the car, and I'd end up climbing into his lap. They didn't cover this kind of agony in advice columns.

His phone rang and he said, "Hey, look at this."

I turned from the window to his iPhone, expecting to recognize someone's name in the caller ID. Instead, there was a picture of the sole of a shoe. Bennett swiped his thumb over the heel, which slid open to reveal a mouthpiece.

"Bennett Stern," he answered in a spylike voice. "We're on the train now. We'll arrive at six o'clock."

He flipped the heel closed and turned to me, grinning.

"You were talking on your shoe phone," I said. "To headquarters! Where'd you get that?"

"Off a dead KAOS agent in East Germany."

I couldn't help myself: I hugged him, then buried my face in his neck. I breathed in the scent of him, savoring every second. Then pressed my lips to his skin and he gasped.

"I'm sorry," I said, pulling away.

"I'm not."

He leaned closer and kissed me. The train trembled and my heart beat faster. My eyes closed and I lost myself in the sweetness of it. We kept our hands to ourselves, like if only our lips touched, then maybe everything would be okay. A false hope, but it made it the sexiest kiss ever, feeling nothing except his lips on mine.

When I regained my sanity, I turned my head to end

the kiss, but that just gave him access to my ear. He nibbled. I melted. Eons later, when I rediscovered my bones, I stood shakily.

"I, um, I'm gonna . . ." I fumbled for my bag. "I think I should sit somewhere else."

With his hands gripping the chair rails, he nodded.

I stumbled over him and found an empty seat, four rows back, next to the window. I leaned my head against the glass and watched the world outside blurring into grayness. The hours passed, and I wondered how much longer we could go on like this. This wasn't some unrequited crush where you didn't know how the boy felt, where if you threw yourself at him, he might recoil. I knew exactly how Bennett felt, and he knew exactly how I felt. We wanted each other, plain and simple.

Okay, maybe not so simple. But I couldn't allow myself to think that there wasn't some solution, and I spent the rest of the train ride trying to figure it out.

As we pulled into Penn Station, Bennett slid into the seat beside me. "Tell me it's worth it," he said. "Tell me this is going to be over soon, and we can be together."

He'd never asked me for reassurance before, not like that. I wanted to comfort him, tell him that everything would definitely be okay. But I owed him the truth.

"It's not just your sister, Bennett," I said. "It's not just finding Neos and killing him."

"What is it, then?" he asked.

As the train squealed to a halt, I looked into his eyes.

"It's you. The you I fell in love with is a ghostkeeper. That's the only you there is. How can I ask you to give that up?"

"I want to," he said. "For you."

But I just shook my head, and we gathered our bags as the other passengers started to exit. I followed Bennett through the station and onto the street. The air was cold and a grim sky peeked between the looming buildings.

Moments later we were in a taxi, heading downtown.

The avenues of Midtown started to narrow, and the taxi turned into a cramped neighborhood of brick buildings and little quaint shop fronts filled with antiques and cool clothing. I tried not to look like a tourist while gawking at everything. Even jaded urbanites gawked sometimes, right?

Bennett told the cabdriver to stop at the corner, and we grabbed our bags and stood on the sidewalk in the powdery snow. My senses flared at the sights and sounds, and I almost staggered under the impact of all the spirits lingering along the streets.

Two male ghosts in navy uniforms passed a flapper from the twenties, who winked gaily at a young ghost who looked like he'd died in some kind of disco accident. The ghosts roamed in packs of two and three, greeting each other and commenting on the snow, and generally acting as though they weren't dead.

"Pretty intense, huh?" Bennett said.

"Wait—is that *Elvis*?"

"What would Elvis be doing here?" he scoffed. "That's just a chubby guy with muttonchops and a white jumpsuit."

He led me down the cobblestoned street, past narrow brownstones with ornate wrought-iron fences and with ancient trees growing between the sidewalks.

"So, is this whole block ghostkeepers?" I said.

"Yeah, mostly people involved with the Knell."

As dusk crept over the rooftops, I watched a ghost boy who looked like Nicholas climb a streetlamp, light a long match, and fiddle with the glass. The lamp lit instantly— but from electricity, not his flame.

"I don't get it," I said. "They're not like the ghosts in Echo Point." Or even the ones I remembered from my childhood, before my parents had my ability suppressed. "It's like they don't know they're dead."

"Maybe it's the street," he said. "Or the Knell, or how many ghostkeepers live here. No one's really sure why, but they almost forget they're ghosts."

We passed a small private park where a few old spirits played chess at tables under the streetlamps. A younger one moved a rook. He was eccentrically dressed and some-how familiar.

I stopped and stared. "Is that . . . ?"

"The actor?" A movie star who'd recently died of an overdose. "Yeah."

"Have you asked if it was suicide or an accident?"

He looked at me. "No."

"Oh, right." Communicating was my thing, not his.

The block dead-ended at a white stone behemoth of a house, with columns and turrets and arches, and things that might've been flying buttresses, for all I knew. It looked like an institution, but there was no sign; instead, ornate iron gates and heavy trees stood guard.

"What did it used to be?" I asked, expecting Bennett to say it belonged to the first governor of New York or a Rockefeller or, I don't know, the pope.

"It's always been the Knell."

We headed toward the gate; then Bennett stopped and gave me a strange look, one I couldn't decipher.

"What?" I asked.

"I should've prepared you." He tilted his head. "I didn't tell you before, because I didn't know how, but there's something inside. You're not going to like it."

"Well, that's nice and cryptic." I took a steadying breath. "It doesn't matter. As long as they help us find Neos and my family."

Then the iron gates swung open and the house received us.

3

A ghost servant stood beside the door, dressed in what I thought was called livery. Bennett and I handed him our coats and I thanked him, but he didn't respond.

"Could he not hear me?" I asked Bennett after the servant drifted away. I was used to ghosts being pleased when I communicated with them.

"He probably could. I told you, they're different here."

"You mean rude."

"I mean different."

"Well, it's pretty *different* that nobody's here to meet us. Don't we have an appointment?"

"They know we're here. They'll send for us when Yoshiro's ready."

So we wandered the halls, waiting for a human to greet us—I mean a *living* human.

One thing you could say about ghostkeepers: they liked their artifacts. The inside of the Knell could've passed for a museum. Not like Bennett's house, which resembled a period-piece movie set; this was more like the Met. Ornate furnishings dotted the immaculate marble floor and left plenty of room for bronze sculptures, oil paintings, and antiquities on pedestals. The lighting was low, protecting the art and Oriental rugs, and creating a fittingly spooky ambience.

I ran a finger along the etching of an ivory box. My skin began to tingle and I quickly pulled my hand away. I sometimes sensed the memories of antiques like these, impressions of the people who once owned them. In the case of my namesake, the first Emma, I actually relived her experience, and I was afraid something like that might happen here.

And sure enough, I sensed something calling to me from one of the rooms. Not a ghost, but an object tugging at my attention.

"Um, Emma?" Bennett said. "Where are you going?"

"I don't know."

I followed my instincts, winding down wood-paneled hallways until I stood in a dark room, almost empty except for a tapestry on one wall and a blue velvet Victorian settee in the middle of the room, inviting you to sit and admire the intricate weaving.

"This is it, isn't it?" I said, mesmerized by the tapestry. "The thing you should've told me about."

"Uh-huh." Bennett grew still, watching me, gauging my reaction.

The tapestry reminded me of the famous Lady and the Unicorn tapestries. We'd had a print of one of them in our hallway when I was a child. The colors and patterns were the same. The rich golds and burgundies, dark blue and forest green, the moons, trees, flowers, even the bunnies. A light-haired woman stood in the middle of this one, dressed in a red medieval gown, a sword held protectively across her body.

But instead of interacting with the animals, she was circled by ghosts in different guises: in human form, wraiths, and what I guessed were ghasts, though I'd never seen one. One of the ghosts was even a serpent, delicately woven into the fabric.

"Is that Emma?" I asked. Because she looked exactly like her—like me.

"Yeah, just not the Emma from Echo Point. This tapestry is centuries older than her, probably medieval European."

My Emma lived in the late 1700s, which meant that this tapestry was almost five hundred years old. "But—"

"She's a mirror image of you," a woman's voice said behind us.

I turned too quickly and caught a glimpse of the woman before the world started tilting. I stumbled, and Bennett took my arm and helped me to the settee. He crouched in front of me, holding my hands in his, his eyes concerned.

"Take a deep breath," the woman told me. "You've had a shock."

"I've got it," Bennett snapped at her. "I'm sorry, Emma. I should've told you. But we don't really know what it is or what it means. And I didn't want you to . . . to take it too seriously."

I touched his shoulder briefly. "It's okay. I'm not sure knowing it was here would've prepared me, anyway. It's not every day you discover you're the reincarnation of Emma the Ghostslayer."

"It's striking, isn't it?" the woman said to Bennett. "Yoshiro says that Emma is the only ghostkeeper who can stop Neos—which is odd, given she's so new to her powers. But when you see her resemblance to the lady in the tapestry, all that power, distilled through the ages, leaping from bloodline to bloodline." She turned to me. "Until finally settling in you. I begin to think Yoshiro's right."

"Who are you?" I asked, eying the woman. She looked about my parents' age, tall and dark haired with hazel eyes. And vaguely familiar. "Do I know you?"

She smiled in surprise. "Actually, yes—though we haven't met since you were a little girl. Or maybe it's simply innate recognition."

"Because we're both ghostkeepers?"

"No," she said, "because we're family."

"I don't have family," I told her. "Only my parents and brother. My grandparents died before I was born, my mom's an only child, and my dad's not in touch with—"

"His sister," she finished.

"Wait," I said. "You're my dad's sister?"

Bennett glared at her. "You never told me this."

She nodded. "I'm your aunt."

"Rachel?" I asked, astonished. She looked a little like my father around the eyes and in the way she smiled.

Her face glowed with pleasure, and she stepped forward like she wanted to hug me. I would've let her, except Bennett was glowering—and I was trying to remember why she and my father weren't in touch anymore.

Instead of the hug, she sat beside me and squeezed my arm. "I'm so pleased to finally meet you—again." She laughed. "The last time I saw you, you were still in diapers."

Great. Just how I wanted Bennett picturing me: in princess-themed Pampers. At least he hadn't kept this from me. The tapestry paled in comparison. Rachel seemed okay and all, but did I really need an unexpected aunt cluttering up my life? I had enough going on with dead friends, ghostly vendettas, and an untouchable boyfriend.

"Do my parents know you're in the Knell?" I asked. "Where are they? Does my brother, Max, know about you?"

"Wait, wait—one question at a time," she said.

"I've got one," Bennett said, his face hard. "Do the others know you're her aunt? I don't like this, Rachel—springing this on Emma without any warning. She's been through enough surprises already."

"This is a family matter."

"It's a Knell matter," he said. "Let's bring this to Yoshiro and William and Gabriel, then we'll *all* hear you answer Emma's questions."

"They know. I wanted a moment to speak with her privately," she said.

"Emma doesn't need—"

I cut him off. "I'm good, Bennett. I want to talk to her. She's family and the only one who hasn't run out on me. Well, if you don't count when I was a baby." Plus, for all I knew she was the key to Max's and my parents' disappearance. "You go ahead; tell them we'll be there soon."

"You sure?"

I gave him a look. I liked how protective he was, but I needed to do this on my own, and I sensed Rachel wouldn't talk with him around.

He smiled wryly, reading my expression. "Okay," he said. "Back in five minutes."

After he left, I turned to Rachel and waited for her to begin, conscious of a vague feeling of disquiet. Maybe due to the tapestry or the proximity of so many ghostkeepers. Or maybe I was just picking up on Rachel's anxiety.

She licked her lips and looked from the tapestry back to me. "Your father didn't take your mother's powers, Emma. Neos did. They—*we* were all working for the Knell, the four of us as a team. Nobody dispelled ghasts better than we did." Her eyes flashed at the memory. "Then your mother and Neos fell in love, and she started losing her powers. When she became a liability, the Knell wanted her out. Neos immersed himself in the old lore, searching for a way to help her regain her abilities, but nothing worked. He even dabbled in Asarum."

"What's that, some kind of satanic rite?"

"It's an herb that boosts ghostkeeping powers. Extremely addictive—and dangerous." She shook her head. "Neos grew more and more distraught and guilty and he started to change. He became . . . twisted. Obsessed with the old lore, with the powers. Finally, your mother left him and started an affair with my brother."

Ick. I held up a hand. "I don't need the details."

"No." She frowned. "It's not something I like to think about, either."

I waited, but she just sat there staring into space. Finally, I said, "And then?"

She jerked slightly. "Oh! Well, your father thought that the Knell mistreated Jana—your mother. Tossing her aside when she wasn't useful anymore."

"And you?" I asked.

"I thought . . . I thought Jana had been unfair to Neos. He loved her so much, he'd lost his mind trying to save her." She licked her lips again. "I tried to get Nathan, your father, to break it off with her."

My parents were the madly-in-love types, as close as any couple I'd ever seen. It had always been obvious to me and Max that their relationship came first, that we were just a by-product. "He'd never do that," I said.

"No," Rachel agreed. "He accused me of only having the Knell's interests at heart, of not caring about him or Jana."

We sat in silence a moment. "You two haven't spoken since I was a baby?" I asked.

"I tried to apologize but . . . in the end, he was right. After we fought, I lost myself in the Knell." She smiled tentatively. "Which is why I'm so happy you're here. You're like a second chance. I never meant to hurt your parents," she said, leaning forward intently. "I loved them. I hope you believe that."

"Sure," I said. Like me and Max. We fought sometimes, but we always loved each other. Even if he did totally bail on me when I needed him most. "Did the lady in the tapestry have a brother who looked like Max? I mean, is that normal, for a ghostkeeper to look so much like her ancestors?"

"She's my ancestor, too." Rachel's gaze grew hard. "I don't look like her. But then—"

She stopped as Bennett came back.

"Yoshiro's ready for us," he said.

I smiled at him, and not only from affection but also from relief. I wasn't sure how I felt about Rachel. I had to admit, I could use an aunt, since my parents were AWOL. But there was something disconcerting about her, like she wasn't quite comfortable in her own skin. Maybe she was just worried that I'd hate her like my father had.

"Are we ready for *him*?" I asked, standing.

"He's quite formidable," Rachel said. "But don't let him intimidate you."

"As long as he can help me, I don't care."

"If he can't help," Bennett said, "nobody can."

"Yoshiro's the heart of the Knell." Rachel put her hand

on my arm, ushering me toward the door. "Well, maybe not the heart—more the brain."

"You're getting a rare audience, meeting him in person," Bennett said. "I've only seen him once. Usually he stays in his archives."

But I wasn't listening; I was staring at Rachel's hand. My skin felt tingly under her palm, almost like I was touching a ghost, and I jerked away.

"I'm sorry." She smiled apologetically as we headed into the hallway. "I don't know why that happens. I'm a communicator, but sometimes my power gives off static shocks. Or spectral shocks, I suppose."

I glanced at Bennett for reassurance, but he seemed preoccupied, like he was marshaling his strength to meet Yoshiro. I wished we could hold hands.

I nodded vaguely at Rachel, caught between my pleasure at reuniting with a long-lost relative and my sense that she wasn't quite . . . normal. Maybe she seemed a little off because she *was* family. I'd need to get used to the idea.

So I decided to like her. Finally, a family member who was still willing to talk to me. That had to be a good thing, right?

As we headed upstairs, Rachel confided about how daunting she found Yoshiro, until we stopped outside a set of elaborately carved wooden double doors. A couple of male ghost servants stood on either side of the door, as though guarding the room. "I don't mean to frighten you," she said. "You'll be fine."

"Emma's not afraid of anything," Bennett said.

I took a deep breath, hoping he was right.

I smiled at one of the ghosts, but he ignored me while the other opened the door. After that, I expected a throne room or something, but Bennett led me into a small chamber, decorated like a library where you'd find Sherlock Holmes solving the case. It was all cherrywood, leatherbound books, and red and gold Oriental rugs with a fire blazing in the ornately carved fireplace.

Three men sat on leather couches, taking in the heat of the fire. They stood as we entered, and the oldest, an Asian man wearing wire-rim glasses, his long gray hair in a ponytail, stepped forward.

"Emma Vaile," he said, subjecting me to an unsmiling inspection. "You are not as impressive as I'd imagined."

"You must be Yoshiro," I said, with a fake smile. "I thought you'd be taller."

Beside him, the dark-haired younger man coughed, smothering a laugh, then introduced himself as Gabriel. He had a Spanish accent, and the sort of smoldering spark of one of those ugly European guys who's somehow incredibly attractive.

"A pleasure to meet you, Emma," he said. For the record, "Emma" sounded really pretty with a Spanish accent.

"Welcome to the Knell," the third man said, a middle-aged black man dressed in intellectual chic. "My name is William. I remember your mother and father fondly."

"Thanks. It's kind of hard to imagine them here."

Yoshiro cleared his throat. "Sit."

I almost said something snotty about barking and rolling over, but Bennett nudged me toward one of the couches. Everyone sat except Yoshiro, who paced for a minute, then turned suddenly and considered me.

"Except for your youth, your likeness to the tapestry is exact."

"And my hairstyle." She looked like me dressed up for a Renaissance fair. "It doesn't mean anything. It's genetics. Probably happens all the time, except other people don't have medieval tapestries lying around."

"Yoshiro believes it's more than that," Gabriel said.

"Your powers are unprecedented," William said. "And your resemblance to at least two dead ghostkeepers is also unprecedented. That's not a coincidence."

"Maybe not. But I'm not the first Emma, I'm not that medieval lady. I'm just a—" I looked at Yoshiro. "An unimpressive girl who doesn't want to battle ghosts and kill wraiths. There're only three things I want. To find my family. Dispel Neos. And to—" I stopped suddenly, and didn't know where to look.

"Yes?" Yoshiro said. "The third thing?"

"To be with me," Bennett said.

Yoshiro made a disgruntled sound. "You are too close." He waved his hands between us. "This is dangerous."

"We're okay," I said. "Thanks for the concern."

"*You* are okay," Yoshiro said. "But you are not the one

in danger. You have a strange way of showing Bennett your regard, by undermining his ability."

This time, my snappy retort dissolved into flushing with embarrassment, and I squirmed a few inches away from Bennett.

Like a hero, Bennett changed the subject. "What have you learned about Neos?"

Yoshiro crossed to the fire and watched the flames, leaving William to answer. "He's something new, something nobody's faced before. Stronger than any of us—except perhaps you, Emma. And except for the Knell, when we all act together."

"What about my parents and brother?"

"They're obsessed with Neos—with stopping him," Gabriel said. "They warned us this might happen. But it's like they've dropped off the face of the earth."

"They knew he'd come back as a ghost?" I don't know why I was surprised. I suppose they must have figured out it was Neos who attacked me as a child. And Aunt Rachel had filled in some of the missing pieces.

"They are not your concern," Yoshiro said, turning. "Not now. You must focus on Neos. He is gathering strength in the Beyond, summoning wraiths and other, even more unwholesome spirits, forcing them to join his crusade."

"Crusade against who?" Bennett asked. "Emma?"

"She's half of it," William said. "The other half is the Knell. That's why we're taking security even more seriously.

Yoshiro hasn't left his archives in weeks, and Gabriel and I don't leave the building anymore."

"So what're we going to do?" I asked.

"We're bringing the veteran teams home," Gabriel said. "And forming new ones."

"Just like the old days," Rachel said, with a glint in her eyes.

"I'll need Bennett on my team," I said. "And Natalie."

William and Yoshiro exchanged a dubious look. Gabriel simply looked on in a gorgeous Spanish manner.

Rachel nodded, though. "Emma's not one of our soldiers. She needs to be close to those she loves." She came and sat beside me. Her proximity unsettled me for some reason, though I was relieved someone was on my side.

"You know that's not wise," Yoshiro told her. "You of all people know that personal feelings undermine a group."

"I won't do it without them," I said.

Everyone looked to Yoshiro, and as he debated, I squirmed in my seat. But it wasn't because I was worried about his answer; something didn't feel right. My skin tingled, in a bad way.

I frowned at Bennett. "Do you feel that?"

He shook his head. "What's wrong?"

"There's a ghost nearby. It's—" My spine felt hot and itchy. "Not a ghost, a wraith."

"*Imposible*," Gabriel said in Spanish. "Wraiths cannot enter the Knell."

Bennett stood and started drawing his power into his fists, a swirl of light glowing through the flesh and bone. "If Emma says there's a wraith, there's a wraith."

"This building is a powerful nexus," William said. "She's probably feeling the—"

"Rachel!" I said, my eyes widening.

She was quiet and attentive, next to me. Scratching furiously at one of her forearms. Bloody scrapes appeared down her skin.

She twitched a smile. "Skin infection. Poison ivy."

But it wasn't a rash. I could see an oily swirl superimposed over her. It shifted and shimmered, then vanished into the lines on her arm like filthy water into a drain. My breath caught, and I pushed my awareness beyond my body, letting my power ripple across the room. Until I found it: a tight knot of fear and pain and insatiable hunger.

"Emma?" Bennett said, his hands glowing with power. "Emma! Where is it?"

"It—it's my aunt," I gasped. "Rachel. There's a wraith inside her."

"There's no way," Gabriel said. "Wraiths can't possess people—and this building is completely shielded. You couldn't detect a ghost here if you were standing at the front gate, much less summon wraiths."

"And Rachel's the most powerful communicator we have," William said. "She would've known if—"

"Hit her," I told Bennett.

"Stop!" Yoshiro shouted.

"She knows," Rachel screeched. "She *knows!*" Her tone verged on insanity.

Bennett narrowed his eyes, and spears of light flew from his fists and slammed into Rachel's chest. Her back arched and she shrieked, an ungodly howl. Her eyes turned milky and sunk into their sockets, while her skin paled to a dead white and cracked like a mud puddle in a heat wave. Deep, jagged fissures formed, as an inky blackness seeped from inside her.

Bennett snarled and poured more energy at Rachel, and she writhed and twisted as she pointed one dead-white arm at Yoshiro, her mouth open in a soundless scream. William and Gabriel sprang to their feet, but my attention was still focused on other ghostly disturbances in the building around us.

Then Rachel made a horrible choking noise, and the insectlike bone of a wraith sprang from her arm and plunged into Yoshiro's chest.

Lightning crackled around Gabriel. In a blaze of power, he compelled her to freeze, the bony wraith-arm still sunk in Yoshiro's chest. "Don't dispel her," he told Bennett. "Or she'll take Yoshiro with her. William, phone the doctor. If I let her go, he'll bleed out. Quickly!"

They froze there in a horrible tableau, with Rachel's wraith-arm impaling Yoshiro's chest, like a poster for a horror film. But with sound: the pained, panting breaths coming from Yoshiro and the squeals of rage from the wraith inside Rachel.

Time seemed to slow, the world closing in until there was nothing but us, locked together in this terrible room, listening to death approach with every gasping breath.

Then I felt them, a burning itch on my skin—more wraiths.

"They're coming," I said. "More of them."

Gabriel didn't move, his power completely focused on the wraith inside Rachel, but the rest of us prepared to meet the new attack. I faced the fireplace, while William crossed toward the door. Bennett stood beside the couch, a lucent spear from his right hand still weakening Rachel, while his left fist sparked with light.

They didn't come from outside. They came from inside Rachel's cracked skin, oozing through the torn flesh in an unearthly black mist.

I'd seen wraiths before, but it wasn't something you got used to. They condensed from the filthy mist into skin hanging like tattered clothing from insectoid skeletons, ectoplasm dripping from their gaping mouths.

William was an amazing communicator. His mental command boomed out, *There is nothing for you here. Leave us! If you stay, we will dispel you.*

His tone held such power and conviction that it almost stopped *me*. But there was no communicating with wraiths; they were too consumed with hunger to listen. They screeched their desires: *Feed, feed, eat the flesh, suck the blood . . .*

William used arcane phrases and a tone of complete command, but the chorus of bloodlust drowned out his words. He crumpled to the floor as a wraith flung itself onto him, bony claws slashing his neck.

I gathered my dispelling energy and twisted it around the wraith attacking William. Like wringing water from a dishcloth, I torqued the wraith until nothing was left but a spray of sticky black blood. William pressed his palm to the wound on his neck and crawled to the old-fashioned phone on the desk, as I spun toward the others.

Gabriel remained frozen in place, straining with the effort of compelling the wraith inside Rachel, keeping it from finishing off Yoshiro. Bennett stood at Gabriel's side, protecting him from the other two wraiths. Light crackled and burst around Bennett as he pierced one but was unable to dispel it completely, while the other attacked Gabriel.

They were losing. I concentrated on dispelling the wraith attacking Bennett, adding my own power to his. The wraith slithered away from him and staggered toward me, claws slashing. Drool from its gaping mouth splashed at my feet like acid, and I waited as it lurched forward. I waited until my palm was an inch from its ribcage, then I unraveled it into smoke.

Gabriel yelled for help, and Bennett spun and saw the wraith at Gabriel's throat. He launched a glowing nimbus of light directly into it.

Too late. Gabriel staggered under the wraith's attack and lost control of the wraith inside Rachel. It pulled its bony arm from Yoshiro's chest. An arc of blood spurted across the room as Yoshiro collapsed to the floor. As Bennett burned his way through the wraith still attacking Gabriel, the one inside Rachel leaped at Bennett from behind.

Its bony arm swung in a lethal arc toward Bennett's unprotected neck, and a wave of blackness rose around me, an almost overwhelming flare of fear, rage, and urgency. From some dark chamber of my heart, I unleashed more force than ever before, a single blast directly into Rachel's chest.

The blast shot through her and exploded against the opposite wall. She stopped dead and her insectlike limb morphed back into a regular arm, as she swayed on her feet.

I caught Rachel as she fell, the wraith leeching from her body. Her skin faded from the unnatural white to a deathly pallor, and her eyes, still sunken, glinted with tears.

She clutched at me. "Forgive me; I couldn't stop him."

"Shhh, you're going to be okay."

"No. You need—," she gasped, "a weapon. To focus your power. It's your only hope. Emma, you need . . ." Her voice faltered.

"Rachel," I said. "Don't go. We just met. I need you—"

"I'm sorry," she whispered. "For everything. You need to end this, Emma. Neos fears you. He sent a siren. To cripple you. She will . . ."

And Rachel died.

4

The Knell doctor arrived within minutes. She checked Yoshiro, but we all knew he was dead. When the wraith-arm had jerked out of his chest, blood had spouted across the room. I'd never get that sight out of my mind.

The doctor treated William's wound, disinfecting and stitching it, then tended Gabriel's and Bennett's cuts and bruises. She looked me over and tsked at my chattering teeth and jittery hands, and the blood splatter on my sweater. She offered a Valium for the shock, but I shook my head.

I'd lost Yoshiro, the only person who knew how to defeat Neos. And I'd lost my newfound aunt in the most gruesome way possible. It's called parricide, the killing of a close relative. Probably not on the SATs, but branded in my mind. I didn't want to dull the pain; I wanted to feel it.

We left the room as the doctor began performing an autopsy on Rachel. She didn't want to move the body, as she'd never autopsied the corpse of a possessed person before. We crossed the hall into a sitting room, where we all sat in stunned silence.

"Wraiths can't possess people," Gabriel finally muttered.

"They can now," Bennett said. "And they can march right into the Knell and kill our leader."

Nobody said anything for a while. Then I said, in a small voice, "What do we do?"

"Stick to the plan," William said. "Build the teams. Start training together and . . ." His voice trailed off.

"And what? Does anyone else know how to beat Neos?"

William didn't answer—his defeated expression spoke loudly enough.

"That's why Neos killed Yoshiro," Gabriel told me. "You and he are the only ones who scared Neos. But Yoshiro was careful; he'd been staying out of sight—until today, to meet you."

Bennett nodded. "So Neos put a wraith in Rachel, and waited for his chance. He killed two of the top four people in the Knell, inside our own stronghold. We need to protect Emma."

"She's no threat to him," Gabriel protested, "not without Yoshiro's guidance."

"You want to bet her life on that?" Bennett said, his jaw clenched. "Because the Knell's done so well with predictions lately. You didn't even know Rachel was possessed."

"It's not that simple," William said. "We can't commit ourselves to Emma before we know what we're facing. Maybe that's what Neos wants us to do."

He and Bennett argued for a few minutes, until I interrupted. "What is wrong with you people? I've been doing
this for like twenty minutes—you're the ones with the
massive headquarters in New York and a thousand years
of practice. I thought you knew what you were doing.
That's why I came."

William rubbed his eyes. "This is something new,
Emma. Your appearance, Neos's bond to you, these wraiths
and possessions. Yoshiro would still be alive if . . ."

"If I hadn't come?"

The doctor knocked and stepped inside before William could answer. Her preliminary autopsy of Rachel
revealed that she would've died within the hour, even if
we hadn't dispelled the wraith inside her. The doctor
shook her head. "But that's all speculative. I've never seen
someone possessed. Her organs are a mess, as if the wraith
grew to fill the cavity of her body—not just a spectral
force, but a physical one."

So, technically, I hadn't killed her. But the act was the
same, the murderous rage I'd felt when I wanted to protect
Bennett, and didn't care who I'd hurt. A burning anger
that came too easily—and felt too good.

I wondered how long she'd been alive with that thing
inside her, using her like a puppet while choking her
to death from within. And what about her last words to
me? Saying that I needed a weapon—and warning me
about a threat, a siren that Neos would send to cripple
me? What was that? Could I even trust her dying words?

I thought about her eyes as she died, the pain and the truth shining in them. At the end, that was her. The real Rachel, my long-lost aunt. Lost again, now.

Bennett and I left after that. There was nothing more to say. Downstairs, we passed the room that held the tapestry, and I couldn't help looking one last time. Was I really the reincarnation of some ghostkeeping legend? The woman's face looked stronger than the one I saw in the mirror; she looked like someone who'd seen terrible things. She looked like someone who'd *done* terrible things. I didn't want to be her, and I definitely didn't want to become her.

And yet, what happened tonight felt like only the beginning. There would be more blood, more pain, more deaths. Things would never be the same again. Why me? Just because I was descended from the person woven into this tapestry? Did my whole life boil down to ancestry? My parents, who'd lied to me. My brother, who'd disappeared. The previous incarnations of me, who'd fought and died.

I looked from the woman's face to the ghosts surrounding her. She looked strong and fierce, but she didn't look happy.

As we descended the imposing front steps of the Knell, I asked Bennett, "Have you ever seen that, a wraith breaking out of a ghostkeeper's body?" I tried to erase the image of Rachel plunging her wraith-arm into Yoshiro's chest, and failed.

"No, that was a first."

"Before she died, Rachel said I needed a weapon."

He turned toward me and assessed the damage—the exhaustion in my eyes, the bloodstains on my clothes, my hands balled into fists. "What you need is a good night's sleep. I booked us a hotel. I knew you wouldn't want to stay here."

We walked through the front gates to the street. Ghosts and ghostkeepers alike watched as we strode through the ancient lane, back to civilization. Word must've gotten out about the attack; they scowled and whispered as we passed.

"They think it's my fault," I said to Bennett.

"Ignore them," he said. "They don't know anything about you."

We took a cab to the hotel, and I fell asleep on the way, my face pressed against the sticky black vinyl. Must've been the aftermath of all that energy I'd exploded into Rachel. Or just the emotional exhaustion of the day.

I blinked blearily when Bennett gently woke me and escorted me into the lobby of an intimate and chic hotel that my mother would've loved. I suddenly yearned for her. She'd never been the comforting sort, but she was at least good for a cuddle when things got this low.

Which was more than I could say for Bennett—we couldn't even hug. Still, when he sat me in a chair while he checked in, I couldn't help wondering if he'd reserved one room or two. And though I knew we shouldn't touch, when he came back with two keycards, my heart sank.

We found my room first, and Bennett waited at the door.

"Will you come in?" I asked. "I don't want to be alone."

"Only for a minute," he said as we went inside. "You need to sleep."

I nodded, relieved that he wasn't deserting me. "Do you mind if I jump in the shower? I need to get out of these clothes and . . . scrub the wraiths off my skin."

"Yeah, I know what you mean. Go ahead."

The bathroom was large, considering the size of the room, with elegant fittings and warm beige tile. There were fluffy white towels and lush bath products, and the whole place felt about a thousand miles from the Knell.

After the shower, I slipped into the gray silk robe I'd packed and applied a little lip gloss—and heard the door to the room close. Had Bennett grown tired of waiting for me? I poked my head out and found him sitting on the chair in a fresh navy T-shirt and jeans, his own hair wet.

"I showered, too," he said. "My room's the next one over. I tried to be quick."

I crossed the floor and stood in front of him. "The first time we met, did you know who I was?"

"You were Max's little sister." He glanced away. "Don't you have pajamas? Something high-necked and flannel?"

"You know what I mean, Bennett. Did you recognize me? Know that I looked like Thatcher's Emma and the one in the tapestry?"

"When I met you, you looked like a geeky little girl in braces."

"I didn't wear braces!"

"No, but you looked like you did."

I narrowed my eyes. "You're trying to change the subject."

He took a steadying breath. "Yes, I recognized you. The lady in the tapestry is legendary, Emma. And you not only share her ancestry, but her name."

I didn't want to ask my next question, but I had to know. "Did the Knell tell you to pretend to be in love with me, so I'd do what they wanted? Is this all a lie?"

"No." He took my hands. "Emma, ever since I met you, I knew I shouldn't care for you. But I did—even then. I couldn't help how I felt. The last thing the Knell wants is for us to be in love. They think I've betrayed them. But I'm sorry, there are powers stronger than ghostkeeping."

I felt my heart loosen as I stared at our interlocked hands. "I just want to touch you."

"Me, too," he said, his voice rough.

I was suddenly aware of my nakedness under my robe. "Couldn't we . . . just once?"

He brought my hands to his lips. "You don't know what you're asking."

"I want to be with you. I want to be who we really are, a girl and a boy who fell in love. For one night, can't we pretend there are no wraiths and no deaths? I want to be a normal girl, who's not worried about anything except if her boyfriend is going to kiss her everywhere she wants to be kissed."

He exhaled, and his warm breath caressed my

fingers—then he pulled me into his lap. I felt his hands, rough and strong on my skin. He kissed my neck and my ear and whispered, "Yes."

I touched him, wanting to hold onto every inch of him, forever.

"Just once." He brushed his lips across my eyelids. "I love you."

And I closed my eyes, overcome by a wave of love and desire and the aching need to be everything for him.

He lifted me into his arms and said, "Where else do you want to be kissed?"

Later, as we lay entwined, he said, "It's not that I don't want to." He ran a fingertip across my brow. "It's just that once won't be enough."

I looked into his bright blue eyes and cuddled closer. "This is perfect."

5

Bennett was gone when I woke the next morning. We'd fallen asleep together, and for the first time since my parents' disappearance, I'd felt safe. Now I snuggled with the empty space where he'd been, trying to recapture the feeling.

He knocked at the door as I finished dressing, and I found him in the hallway holding two steaming cups. He handed me one, and I smelled a red-eye chai. I smiled and rose on tiptoes to kiss him, but he brushed past me into the room.

"The train leaves in half an hour," he said. "You ready?"

My heart sank. The old Bennett was back, the cold, impenetrable Bennett who always tried to live up to his last name: Stern.

"Everything's changed," I said. "Can we talk about what happened last night?"

"There's nothing to say."

"Well, what're we going to do?" We couldn't go back to not touching each other.

"What is there to do? You said it yourself, you fell in love with a ghostkeeper. That's what I am." He looked me in the eye. "That's what I'll always be."

I felt like he'd slapped me. If he planned to stay a ghost-keeper, that meant he couldn't be with me. That meant he didn't *want* to be with me—even after last night.

I couldn't deal with it. I didn't know how to talk to him without getting more hurt, so I turned my back and breathed until I was sure I wouldn't start crying. Then I focused on packing my suitcase. Bennett waited in the hall as my gaze swept the room one last time. It looked so ordinary, even though everything was different—at least for me. I saw the rumpled bedsheets and blinked away tears of humiliation and disappointment. How could I have thought everything was perfect when Bennett didn't feel the same? My red-eye chai sat untouched on the dresser as I shut the door, and left that room behind me forever.

We walked to the train station. I didn't see the buildings around me. I didn't see the cars in the street. I was blind and numb and empty.

But deep inside, I felt a flicker of hope. I knew he was scared, but he couldn't give me the silent treatment for the whole train trip. We'd talk, we'd figure this out. Even if we couldn't be together right now, we could go back to the way things were before. Not touching, but still happy with each other. Still in love.

Except when we got to the platform, he pulled out the ticket. One ticket.

"Where's yours?" I said.

"I'm not going back with you."

Blood rushed to my head. "What? Why not?"

"I'm needed here."

"You're needed *there*. We need you. *I* need you."

"Emma, I can't—don't you see?" he said desperately. "Everything *has* changed. I can't go back to not touching you. I can't look at you without wanting to . . ." He shook his head. "I can't live with you in Echo Point and not sneak into your bedroom every night. I can't watch you giggling with Natalie or playing marbles with Nicholas or sighing over one of Anatole's croissants and not want to kiss you. I can't."

"I won't do those things. I'll—"

"I can't even think—" He ran his fingers through his hair. "Just standing with you in a train station, looking like you want to cry, and I can't think."

"We can make it work. I promise, we'll—"

"No, Emma. It's impossible."

"Impossible? We slay ghosts, Bennett."

"That's just it. I'm good; I'm one of the best dispellers there is. Whenever there was a truly nasty ghast, the Knell sent *me* out."

"I know how strong you are; I've seen you in action. You saved me from Neos once."

"That was before I let myself touch you. I'm losing my powers, Emma. I can feel it already. I woke up this morning and . . . it's already happening, and we didn't even—you're too much. What happens if I'm with you, and I can't hold myself back? I might lose my ability to dispel, and how would I explain that to my parents—I can't find my sister's killer because I'm in love? It's over, Emma. I'm sorry, but I can't do this."

The finality in his voice stole my words. I just stood there watching him through tear-blurred eyes. The train pulled in, and the screeching of the brakes echoed the weeping in my head.

Bennett helped me board, lugging my suitcase into the compartment overhead. He was right; everything he said was true. I had no solution, I had no clue. I didn't know anything except this: he loved me, and I loved him.

Bennett said, "Stay safe."

I nodded, unable to handle looking at him.

Then he was gone.

The train pulled from the station, and I didn't bother checking outside to see if he was watching. No romantic, lingering looks for us. No blown kisses, no promises to meet again. No nothing.

I froze all the way back to Echo Point, shivering in my wool coat even though the train was heated, hating the gray November sky and barren New England landscape. Wishing I was back in California—before my parents disappeared, before my best friend, Abby, deserted me, before Bennett had walked back into my life, and before I'd ever heard the word *ghostkeeping*.

But I didn't cry. Not until the train pulled into Boston

and I saw Natalie waiting for me at the station, concern etched into her face. Bennett had obviously called and prepared her. I stumbled from the train and fell into her arms, weeping.

We took a taxi back to Echo Point. Natalie cradled me as I explained everything to her, not caring that the driver could overhear. "He hates me," I said.

"He doesn't hate you, Emma. Just the opposite."

"It's all my fault," I said. "If I'd just let him go to his own room . . ."

"Emma, stop blaming yourself. It was inevitable. There's nothing you could've done differently."

I took a deep, shuddering breath. "Why doesn't that help?"

"Because it's still a heartache. And nothing makes you want to die more than that."

When I woke on Wednesday, a sparky little fire was blazing in the fireplace in my bedroom, no doubt thanks to Nicholas. All my clothes were put away, and Celeste had hung my clean uniform on the wardrobe door. I glanced at the clock on the mantel, and buried my head under the covers.

I'd taken two days off from school, and was going to take a third. I couldn't face Harry and Sara and all the other kids who blamed me for Coby's death. Not this week. Not after losing Bennett. This week was for wallowing in self-pity, eating junk food, and sleeping myself into oblivion.

I lay in the overheated darkness until a knock sounded at my window. I peeked from under the covers and saw Coby hovering outside.

When he saw me, he shimmered into existence beside my bed.

You're getting good at that, I said, sitting up in bed.

I've got a lot of time on my hands, he said.

I didn't know what to say to that, so I started chewing on my thumbnail.

I've been to my parents', he said. *You didn't tell me they wouldn't be able to see me.*

I— It hadn't occurred to me that you'd think they would. They're not ghostkeepers.

Ghostkeepers, right. He sprawled on the chair. *God, that's so lame.*

Yeah.

I saw Harry and Sara, he said.

They hate me now.

He didn't seem to care. *Harry's drinking again.*

What?

He starts first thing in the morning. It's bad, Emma. Keeps a silver flask in his coat pocket.

Damn, I said. *What about Sara?*

An unreadable expression flicked across his narrow, pale face. *Did you know she was in love with me?*

Yeah, I answered softly.

You did?

She made me promise not to hurt you, I said. *Instead, I got you killed.*

How could she not tell me? If I'd known— He shook his head. *It doesn't matter. You have to help them.*

They won't even speak to me. I don't know what I'm supposed to do.

Well, figure it out, or you're going to have two more dead friends on your hands.

With that parting shot, he dematerialized. Had he only come to make me feel guilty? If so, it had worked.

I huddled under the covers again. I didn't want to think about Harry and Sara or Coby's parents. I didn't want to think about anything except Bennett. I closed my eyes and returned to that moment when he was beside me, and everything had been perfect. I imagined his eyes and his hands and the little scar on his back that a ghast had left him. I remembered his voice and mouth and the things he said that made me thrill and blush at the same time.

But he wasn't there. He'd left me, just like everyone else. Maybe my mother was right, and I couldn't trust him. I let the sadness wash over me and began to cry.

And then I must've fallen back asleep, because I dreamed not of Bennett, but of a woman's face. In her early twenties, she had short dark hair, wide-set eyes, and scarlet red lipstick. Her brown eyes were deep wells of warmth and comfort, and I fell into them, like a vat of hot chocolate. Her voice soothed me like a lullaby, or the refrain of a favorite song, sweet and familiar and rhythmic.

"Who are you?" I asked in my dream.

A sense of warmth and security spread through me as she continued to hum. I didn't need ghostkeepers or my ring, or my powers. I didn't need Bennett—

I jerked in bed and woke, like being surprised by a dream of falling. That last part had startled my conscious mind, forcing me to wake. Because it wasn't true. I needed him. And no crazy dream was going to change that. Now, if only I could trust him.

I lay in bed until I heard footsteps in the hall, and Natalie burst into the room. "You're not out of bed yet?"

"Yes, I am," I said, from under the comforter.

"It's time for school."

"I'm not going," I mumbled.

She stripped the covers from the bed. "Yes, you are."

"Natalie!" I tried to wrestle the covers back, but she pulled them out of reach.

"Enough's enough. Get in the shower. Right now, young lady."

I curled into a fetal position. "You're mean."

"It's for your own good," she said, tossing me my bathrobe. "I know you're upset, but you're not a wallower, Em."

"What am I, then?" I seriously didn't know sometimes.

"Really? I need to go into how you've killed wraiths and fought off Neos, the most powerful ghost anyone has ever seen? Yeah, your heart is broken, but when you get hit, you're the girl who gets back up again."

We were both silent a moment as I digested this. I grumbled at her, but took a quick shower and got dressed. Natalie helped me accessorize—a major art form at Thatcher—and we headed outside in record time to walk the three blocks to school.

I bit into the toast with peanut butter that Anatole had handed me on the way out the door.

"One hundred sixty calories," Natalie said.

"What? My toast?" I shook my head. "Don't do that. You're going to give me a complex."

"I can't help it—I was a fat twelve-year-old. The Kingdomers frowned on gluttony, and I was a rebel."

The Kingdomers were a religious sect that Natalie's parents belonged to. They hated ghostkeepers—her mother had been one—and basically tried to waterboard Natalie's summoning abilities out of her. I hated to think what kind of diet they'd put her on.

"Well, it's safe to eat now," I said, handing her half my toast. She could stand to gain a few pounds.

She looked at me hesitantly, then bit into the toast. "Yummy," she said, through a mouthful of peanut butter.

"The devil's work always tastes delicious," I said.

As we approached the gates to Thatcher, my trepidation returned. There was Coby, sitting on the surrounding stone wall, staring morosely at the other kids as they passed by. Coby was the first person I'd met when I transferred here, and had quickly become the one friend I could always rely on. Whenever I needed him, he'd been there. We always met at these gates in the morning and walked in together. I wasn't sure how I was going to get through school without him. Yeah, he was still here for me. But as a ghost. And no matter how much I wanted things to be the same, they weren't.

Natalie noticed him and smiled.

How come she can see me? he asked.

She's a ghostkeeper.

But he wasn't paying attention. His eyes were on Sara, who was walking with Harry from the parking lot. Harry staggered on the flagstone path and Sara caught his arm. They both looked worn and tired, as though all the life had gone out of them.

Look at Harry, Coby said. *Drunk already. And Sara's not much better. They need your help, Emma.*

"Let's go," I said to Natalie, ignoring Coby. I dragged her through the gates.

"Did you talk to him?" she asked. She couldn't hear me communicate with Coby. "Stop yanking me."

"Yes, I talked to him."

"What'd he say?"

"Not much," I answered.

Emma, Coby scolded from behind me.

They don't want my help, I said. And I wasn't ready to talk to them. I couldn't be brave all the time. Hey, at least I'd shown up at school. I couldn't confront Harry about his drinking or beg Sara for forgiveness—it was too soon; the wounds were still raw. So I turned my back to them and kept walking.

I tried to avoid Harry, but he cornered me and Natalie in a crowd of other girls in the hallway outside of Latin.

"Good morning, ladies," he said, with a vulpine smile. Then added, "And Emma."

"Ha-ha," Natalie said.

"Oh, I'm extremely witty," Harry said. "And quite the charmer." His voice was low and measured, and not even slightly slurred—but somehow he still seemed drunk. "However, I seem to have misplaced my ability to give a crap. Perhaps you've seen it, Emma. I called it Coby."

"You're not the only one who misses him," Natalie said.

"But Emma is the only one who misplaced him." He tsked at me. "Very clumsy."

"I didn't—" I felt my face redden. "I loved him, too, Harry. I wish—I wish none of this ever happened."

"If wishes were horses, Emma, you'd still be the bitch who killed my best friend." He turned to Natalie. "So, are you going to sit with me, or with QBK?"

"QBK?" Natalie said. "What's that?"

"Quarterback Killer. Catchy, don't you think?"

I swallowed. "It's okay; you can sit with him. It doesn't matter," I mumbled. "Your life is going to be hell if you stick with me."

"At least you've got a life," Harry said as he pushed past us, shoving me into the door.

"Ow," I said, rubbing my arm.

"Suck it up, Em," Natalie said, with false cheer. "The fun is only beginning."

"Thanks." We took our seats. "Martha told me you'd be a true friend. I doubt she realized how much I'd need you."

The teacher closed the door and crossed to the front of the room, firing questions at us in Latin.

"Ego requiro suus."* Natalie whispered.

"Mihi quoque."**

After Latin, I shuffled off to my next class, staring at the ground, trying to avoid the accusatory glances and the "accidental" bumps.

Trig was the hardest; I dreaded seeing Coby's empty desk beside mine. But when I entered the classroom, I discovered him in his old seat.

Really? I plopped down next to him. *Trig's the last place I'll go when I'm dead.*

I didn't come for the math.

For what, then? My charming personality?

He didn't look amused. *You talk to Harry yet?*

Yeah, he's got a new nickname for me. QBK.

---

* I miss her.

** Me, too.

Coby thought for a second, then snorted in his ghostly way. *He's a mean drunk. Always was. He called me Cheese for six months.*

Why Cheese?

Because I hated it. He quieted for a minute, watching Mr. Sakolsky write a problem on the board. *Emma, he needs you.*

He can't stand me, I said, scrawling random numbers in my notebook.

I didn't say he liked you.

How am I supposed to help someone who hates me?

You raised me from the dead. I think talking with a drunk is within your— Coby startled suddenly. *Who are you?*

Edmund, the man in the brown suit, had flickered into existence beside us. He nodded his head in greeting.

Coby, meet Edmund, I said. *He used to teach in this room. He's the one who helped me figure out I was a ghostkeeper.*

You're the one Neos killed, Edmund said, eying Coby curiously. *He'd only killed ghostkeepers before you. They don't come back, you know.*

Coby glanced at me, his brow knit. *So if you die . . . ?*

Yeah, I said, keeping my hand firmly on the desk when Sakolsky asked for volunteers to solve a problem on the board. *If Neos kills me, you won't see me again.*

We're going to find him first, Coby said. *We'll do the killing.*

Such ferocity! Edmund said, with a slight smile. *But you know, Coby, one must take care when speaking about . . . him. Especially with threats. He's turning the Beyond into his own personal property. And if one doesn't know one's way . . .*

Hmm. It hadn't occurred to me that Coby could use some kind of mentor. Someone to show him around the place. Teach him how to be a ghost.

Maybe you can show him, I said. *I didn't know when I summoned him that—*

Emma summoned you? Edmund interrupted with surprise. *That explains why you shine so brightly. I thought I sensed someone new here this morning, a powerful spirit. I'd been quite alarmed, but it must've been you. Yes, yes, you must allow me to show you the possibilities of the Beyond.*

Coby gave me a look like, is this guy for real? And Edmund *was* sort of a nutball—he had, after all, been a high school teacher—but he knew a lot and he hadn't given me any reason not to trust him.

So I said, *I'll see you later.*

Promise you'll speak to Harry.

I will, I said. But I didn't say when.

I watched them disappear into the ether, and Mr. Sakolsky scolded me for staring out the window. The whole class turned to shoot me dirty looks, so I buried myself in the intricacies of trigonometry, wishing all my problems had such concrete solutions.

After class, I retreated to my locker. Thatcher's lockers were clustered in lounges—with leather club chairs, potted plants, and oil paintings—that were meant to be study rooms, but were more like hangouts. There was a certain cachet to each lounge, and heavy negotiating for the best of them. Since I started the school year late, I'd been assigned a nerdy lounge offering little in decor beyond an uncomfortable vinyl couch and a molting fica tree, which discouraged lingering.

Today I was grateful for the solitude when I found a Barbie doll hanging inside my locker. Someone had sheared its blond hair to look like my choppy, short hair-cut, dressed her in a plaid school uniform—and strung her tie into a noose.

It bothered me more than it should've. It was malevo-lent and cruel and whoever had put it there (Harry!) had no idea how close I'd come to death that night Coby had been killed.

I untied Barbie and buried her in the trash. Then I thought for a second and wasn't sure if trashing my like-ness was a good idea. So I dug her out, straightened her uniform, and tidied her hair. She looked pretty unim-pressed by the rough treatment, so I put her in my bag, and decided to emulate her self-confident serenity.

6

Much to my chagrin, Fencing was a required course at Thatcher. Not that I wasn't good with a sword, but I fought like a barroom brawler. There's nothing elegant about fighting a wraith, which was why I was terrible at fencing. Sure, I could beat anyone in class in a real swordfight, but I couldn't get a feel for the rules and intricacies of the exhibition sport.

I trudged downstairs and into the only room at Thatcher that looked like it belonged in a regular school: the girls' locker room. The floors were gray concrete, the lockers public-school brown. I was late, and slipped into my fencing whites as the bell rang.

In the gym, the coach paired me with Sara. "She'll go easy on you."

"Oh!" I said. "No. Actually, she's—"

"Delighted," said Sara, prowling in front of me.

She was beautiful in her anger, mahogany locks twirling about her shoulders as though they were mad, too.

Her color was high and her voice low—even rougher than usual, like she'd worn herself out crying over Coby.

She lowered into en garde position, and I made a half-hearted effort to defend myself.

She lunged and I riposted, back and forth down the mat. Well, mostly back, because I wasn't attacking, just defending.

"Would you fight?" she said.

"I don't want to fight you."

"You promised"—she executed a perfect coupé—"you wouldn't hurt him."

I fell back. "I'm sorry."

"You're *sorry*? He's dead, and you're sorry."

"I couldn't—" I swallowed. "There was nothing I could do."

"Do you really believe that?"

The point of my foil drifted downward. "No."

"Neither do I."

And with that, she stabbed me in the chest . . . and then she just lost it. A horrible, wracking sob burst from her chest, and she started flailing at me with the foil like it was a riding crop.

I guess I just stood there.

In a minute, Coach noticed and started screaming at Sara. She banished her to the bench, threatening disciplinary action, but Sara just hurled her foil across the room and shoved into the locker room.

The ghost jocks—two teenage boys whose mission in

death seemed to be heckling me—shimmered into being on the bleachers.

That Sara has great form, the dark-haired one said.

Indeed, the other agreed. *And she fences well, too.*

Then they high-fived each other over their smarminess.

I slunk over to the bleachers on the other side of the room, and in a minute Natalie came and sat beside me.

"Are you okay?" she asked.

"I'm fine," I said.

"You could've defended yourself."

"I deserved it," I said.

"No, Emma, that's where you're wrong."

Someone stole my lunch. My locker had definitely been compromised, and I vowed to carry a bigger bag, so I wouldn't have to use it anymore. Anatole always packed loads too much, so Natalie shared with me.

We sat in the corner of the cafeteria, which was nothing like the cafeterias I'd grown up with. It was more like a quaint dining room. There were no gray-haired lunch ladies slopping peas into trays, just the unscrewing of thermoses and quiet tinkling of silverware brought from home. Not wanting to call attention to myself, I answered Natalie's forays into conversation with monosyllables. I was reminding myself of Bennett.

"I like the lemon dressing on the salad."

"Mm."

"Good grapes."

"Yup."

"Want some more chicken?"

"Nope."

"You're thinking about Bennett, aren't you?"

"Maybe."

I glanced up and saw Sara and Harry frowning at me from across the room. They were backlit by the windows, and for once the sun was shining, making them look like avenging angels. I just couldn't take it anymore.

"I've gotta go," I told Natalie. I stood and helped her pack up the remains of the lunch, then started for the door.

I almost made it. I was three steps away when a foot came out from one of the tables and tripped me. I fell to my knees and, as though I was still six years old, I almost burst into tears.

"This is pathetic," Natalie said, standing and facing the rest of the cafeteria. "I'm only going to say this once. Emma is not responsible for Coby's death. He almost killed her by tying her to that torture device you people call a monument. She barely escaped, then Coby took his own life. She doesn't deserve this. It's not her fault he's dead. Mourn him, but don't smite her. Coby wouldn't have wanted that."

When she'd finished, she led me from the room with her back erect and head high, like a queen having issued her edict.

"You were awesome," I said in the hallway outside. "I've never heard anyone use the word *smite*."

She grinned. "Old habits die hard." Then she grew serious. "This is going to blow over, Em. Things will get better."

"I know," I said.

But in Western Civ, someone had carved *QBK* into my desk. I just wished I knew *when* they'd get better.

After school, I dragged my laptop into the museum kitchen. I bit into an apple and sat in the breakfast nook, scanning my messages. Hoping to hear from Bennett.

He hadn't e-mailed, of course—but Abby had. Which surprised me, because she'd kind of deserted me. She was a ghostkeeper, too. Sort of. We'd been best friends forever, until she'd hooked up with Max last summer. That's when she'd discovered she could summon ghosts, though I didn't know at the time, because I was still in the dark about my own powers.

I guess Max had freaked out, accused Abby of stealing his powers, and dumped her. But Abby hated seeing ghosts, and was trying to lose her powers altogether. She was weak, so if anything, Max would've absorbed her abilities. But they'd both acted like drama queens, so that simple solution had never occurred to them.

Hey Emma,

I can't see ghosts anymore!!!

This cute guy knocked on my dorm-room door

last night and offered to cure me. I kind of freaked out, because I didn't understand how he could know that I saw ghosts. But they were still coming to me in my dreams, and I was just desperate enough to believe him.

It worked, Emma. We held hands and he said some crazy ritual and I could feel all that power draining from me. And now I can't see ghosts anymore. They're gone!

Which means we can be friends again, even if you're in Massachusetts and still part of that creepy ghost world. I'm just glad it's over. I worry about you. The guy wouldn't leave his name or number or anything, but I hope he finds you. Maybe he can cure you, too.

And if you ever need me, I'm here——just not about this stuff! Anyway, I thought you should know that there's hope . . .

Love,

Abby

Wait. What? Some guy had stripped her powers? That sounded a little too much like Neos for comfort—though nobody would call him cute. Maybe he'd possessed another body to steal her power? Had he approached Abby because of me?

So many questions, and nobody to ask for answers. Normally, I'd be on the phone to Bennett, but not now.

Should I call Gabriel or William? I barely knew them, and they already blamed me for everything.

Abby's e-mail left a bad taste in my mouth. She was there if I needed her . . . just not about the only stuff I might actually need help with? Everything I was going through—the deaths of my friends, my family disappearing, Rachel dying, Bennett leaving—was because I could control ghosts. How could she expect me to act like it was nothing, like I was just some normal girl?

Because I wasn't, not anymore. Maybe I never had been.

I didn't delete the e-mail, but I didn't respond, either. My mother always warned me that friends grew apart. I just wasn't prepared for how hard it would be. How hard everything would be.

I stared through the window, taking stock. According to Rachel, I needed a weapon to focus my powers and to watch out for some mysterious siren. Coby wanted me to talk to Harry and Sara, and I needed to figure out who'd taken Abby's abilities. I also needed to wait for my team, so I could stop Neos before he killed anyone else.

That was a lot for one To Do list. What I really needed was food.

I raided the pantry for Anatole's chocolate-chip shortbread. Then googled "siren" and found a bunch of stuff about the Greek myth. Since I wasn't a sailor and couldn't be lured to crash my ship against the rocky coastline, it wasn't helpful.

I read the rest of my e-mail, which was just spam and hate mail from kids at school about Coby. I deleted them unread. The subject lines were bad enough. I skimmed some of my favorite blogs, but nothing satisfied. I was antsy, and wished I knew how to blow off steam like Natalie. I wasn't a runner like her . . . but maybe there was another way.

I went upstairs and changed into a T-shirt and leggings, then went into Bennett's dad's study for one of the swords that hung on his wall. Across the hall in the ballroom, I closed the gauzy curtains and plinked a few keys on the grand piano.

The Rake appeared before I summoned him, as if he knew that I needed him. He was Bennett's namesake and Emma's lover—the one who'd lived at Thatcher. I called him the Rake because he was an eighteenth-century bad boy with a rough exterior that masked the sensitive soul underneath. And he was awesome with a sword, because rakes were always fighting duels and such; at least, that's what I'd learned from my mother's old romance novels.

I saw a flash of motion and caught a glimpse of him in his open-necked dress shirt, buff-colored pants, and riding boots, before his rapier slashed toward me.

I yelped and backpedaled. *Hey! I'm not ready!*

Such is life, he said with a crooked grin, as the flat of his blade smacked my elbow.

Pain flared in my arm, and I swore and switched the sword to my left hand and went on the attack. He lifted an eyebrow, which was about the only sign of approval he ever showed, and parried my furious blows.

Our swords caught and he said, *You're getting sloppy.*

I had a long day, okay?

I'm sure Neos will wait until you're fully rested to—

He shoved me across the parquet floor, then kicked my ankle with the edge of his boot. I grunted and stumbled— then dropped under his flashing sword and sliced for his knee. His blade barely caught mine, and his eyebrow lifted fractionally again. Then he pushed me down with his knee and I rolled backward and sprang to my feet just in time to block another blow.

We sparred for an hour, back and forth across the floor, until my arms ached and my breath came in gasps. It was so much better than fencing class. I could grip the sword how I wanted, forget the rules, and practice with someone who actually knew what they were doing. Until I was exhausted.

Enough, enough, I said. *Stop.*

He sheathed his sword and stared at me, his aristocratic face full of disapproval. I'd once checked the museum's records for his death notice: 1792 at the age of forty-three. His wife had died during the birth of their second child, and he'd never married the other Emma. I guess that was enough to keep anyone grumpy in the afterlife.

What? I said, breathing heavily. *I'm having a bad day and I'm tired.*

This is nothing, he said. *I'm not trying to kill you. Not like Neos and his wraiths. You have to be prepared, Emma. I want you to live.*

Unlike his Emma, the first Emma of Echo Point, who'd tried to take her own life to save his. He'd killed her, instead, because if a ghostkeeper kills herself, she doesn't die, but wanders the Beyond forever, her sanity slowly crumbling through eternity. That's what happened to Neos.

There was another Emma, I said. *Before yours. She's woven into a tapestry at the Knell.*

I'm not surprised.

Why not? I was.

I suspect that you are . . . not reborn, precisely. I think that a ghostkeeper of exceptional ability—and your face—arrives at the great turning points. Like right now, fighting for control of the Beyond.

I flopped onto the piano bench. *But no pressure, right?*

A great deal of pressure, he said, ignoring my sarcasm. *And you're losing focus. You're better than that.*

I'm tired. And now Bennett's gone . . . I bit my lip, trying not to cry. *Do you think there was another Bennett, too? Before you? Did the Emma in the tapestry love another one of you? Were they doomed, as well?*

He moved to lay a hand on mine, then stopped, knowing he'd burn me. *You have to put that aside, Emma. Neos grows more powerful every day. You must learn to protect yourself.*

I sighed. He was right. I stood and held my sword at the ready. *Yeah, my aunt told me I need a weapon to focus my powers. I'm not sure how I'm going to get around with a sword, but it's the only thing I've got.*

To focus? he said. *What do you mean?*

So I told him the whole story about Rachel and the wraiths, plinking absently at the piano as he paced and listened.

When I finished, he shook his head. *You're quick and agile, but you don't have the build for swordfighting. You're too small. A man will overpower you every time.*

I wanted to argue. To sit him down and make him watch old episodes of *Xena*. But I wasn't exactly a warrior princess, and he was right, I hadn't been able to overpower Neos, because he was too strong in Coby's body.

The Rake put his boot on the bench beside me and reached inside for a hidden knife. *What you need is a dagger. It'll allow you to move close and fast, strengths not available to wraiths or Neos.*

I reached for his knife, but he pulled it away. *Not just any dagger—you need* her *dagger.*

Emma's? Where is it?

He hesitated, and his eyes grew distant. *The men who wanted to kill Emma hid her dagger in an unconsecrated cemetery, a mass grave for criminals and heathens.*

So I need to . . . dig it up? Gross.

That's not the problem. The dagger is bait for a trap. The men wanted to lure Emma there so the ghasts would kill her.

Great. Sounds like good times, I said. *Where is it?*

In my day, it was called the Crossing.

The Crossing? I'd seen that name before, on one of my endless walks through the village. *You mean, like, that playground?*

He gave me directions, and sure enough, they'd built a playground over an unconsecrated cemetery. First a ducking chair as a tourist attraction, and now a kids' playground over dead bodies. You had to love Echo Point.

Don't go alone, he said. *The ghasts will be hungry.*

7

I found Natalie in her room upstairs, changing after her run.

"I need a favor," I said.

"You won't fit in my jeans," she said, pulling on a pale blue wool sweater. "And your feet are way too big for my shoes."

"Okay," I said. "First, I would so fit in your jeans. And second—"

"Your butt's bigger," she said, zipping her pants with attitude.

Maybe a little bigger, but she didn't need to rub it in. "What is up with you?" I said.

"What? I didn't say it was *too* big."

"Natalie. What's wrong?"

She refused to tell me—for about ten seconds. Then she said, "I like it here. I like my room, I like that Nicholas lays fires and Celeste does the laundry, and that Anatole tries to woo me with his fatty foods. I like Echo Point and

Thatcher, even if everyone hates you at the moment. I guess I'm just waiting for the other shoe to drop. This is the closest I've been to home in a long time."

"Well, you're staying. The Knell said you could be on my team."

"I know, but Bennett's gone. They're not going to let us live here without him. Two minors living alone in a museum?"

"We're not alone. There are—"

"Ghosts."

"Oh. Yeah."

I didn't want to think about Bennett being gone and whether that meant Natalie and I could no longer stay in the house. I liked it here, too, and didn't want to leave. And I really didn't want to agonize over how a guy who says he loves you isn't supposed to desert you. I was trying to put Bennett out of my mind.

So I said, "Want to go mess around with some ghasts?"

Natalie perked up. "Can we?"

"You're not scared?"

"Why would I be scared? I've got you around to dispel them. This'll be fun."

I wasn't sure how other ghostkeepers traveled to fight a couple of ancient ghasts, but Natalie and I walked, and by the time we got there it was dusk.

"In the playground?" Natalie asked. "Are you sure there are ghosts here? How come nobody's felt them before?"

I nodded. "That's what, um, Edmund told me."

I didn't know how to explain the Rake to Natalie. Yeah, she'd understand that he was a ghost, but she'd want to summon him all the time, which he'd hate. Plus, I kind of liked having him to myself.

The playground was in the corner of a town park, and we crossed the street and followed a gravel path past the oak trees where people tossed tennis balls for their dogs during the day.

I shivered in my peacoat. "I don't like the weather here."

"You Californians are wusses." She eyed the slides and swings.

"I never noticed how creepy playgrounds look after dark." I looked around. "Maybe we should come back."

"No way, man. It only makes it more fun." Natalie was the girl who goes naked in the Jacuzzi and takes the dare instead fibbing about the truth. Ghasts at dusk were not going to intimidate her. "Here goes," she said.

Natalie closed her eyes, and I felt their spirits before she even finished, like needles on my skin. I'd never dealt with ghasts before. They weren't as dangerous as wraiths, but I still felt their twistedness.

"Wait," I blurted. "I'm not ready."

"Too late," Natalie said, opening her eyes. "They're here."

They rose from the ground beside the drinking fountain, as if awakened from a deep slumber. Their heads swayed as they scanned and sniffed for the reason they'd been summoned. They didn't look like wraiths, with tattered skin and hollow eyes, but like regular ghosts, in bad costumes, except gray, like they'd stepped out of an old black-and-white film.

"They look harmless," I said, but the Rake had mentioned a trap.

"Looks are deceiving," Natalie said.

There were two of them, both male, both dressed like the Rake, only less tailored and elegant. They swiveled toward Natalie and me, bared their teeth, and flew at us.

"Okay," Natalie said. "Your turn."

"What?"

"I can only summon them, Emma. You have to dispel them."

I panicked. "I don't know how!"

"What are you talking about? You're Emma frickin' Vaile—you know everything!"

"Run!" I yelled. "Natalie, run!"

Too late—the burly ghast knocked her to the ground.

"Emma!" she screamed. "Do something!"

But I couldn't think; I couldn't remember how to gather my power. I just stood there with an odd humming in my mind.

Natalie screamed and turned her head as the ghast drooled over her. The drool fell into the sandbox and sizzled.

Sizzling drool that would burn straight through Natalie's flesh. That cleared my mind.

I reached out to the ghast. *Stop! She is nothing to you. She is no threat. Leave her!*

He hesitated, and Natalie rolled away. I started to compel him further, when the lankier ghast hit me like a wrecking ball, smashing me into the side of the seesaw. As I struggled to catch my breath, the lanky ghast screeched so piercingly that I was surprised my ears didn't bleed.

The ghast bent me backward over the metal seesaw, which bounced up and down. I couldn't touch the ground as he pressed his hands into my throat, trying to burn me. The sudden shock of pain woke my power, and I centered his spectral gray head between my palms and loosed a blast of energy that scrambled whatever was left of his brain. He lurched away from me, hardly able to stay on his feet.

"Emma!" Natalie called out. "A little help!"

I turned and saw her struggling beneath the burly ghast. With a flicker of thought, I compelled him to leave Natalie alone and join the other ghast, now whimpering inside a spiderweb climbing structure made of rope. He jerkily walked away, like an animated scarecrow, and stepped into the web.

I pulled Natalie to her feet. "Are you all right?" My back was to the ghasts, but my mind was still engaged, feeling their energy, compelling them to stay where they were.

Natalie examined the holes in her parka where the ghast's drool had made contact. "Fantastic. What happened to you?"

"I don't know. Nerves? I froze, I guess."

"Well, as long as you snapped out of it." She glanced toward the ghasts and taunted them. "Not so tough now, are you?"

"Natalie. I think there's more." Another presence tugged at the edge of my mind.

"Oh God!" Natalie said, her voice sharp with fear. "Look!"

The ground beneath the tire swing bulged, and a mound of dirt erupted from the wood chips. A billow of black smoke emerged and twined into a ghast, twice as big as the other two, with oversized hands and feet, long gray hair, and a beard. His mouth opened unnaturally wide, like a snake with unhinged jaws, as he wafted toward us.

"Looks like we sprang the trap," Natalie said.

The humming returned to my mind, and with a jolt of fear I realized that this was too much for me. "I can't control that thing and compel the others at the same time."

"So, run again?" she asked.

"Yeah," I squeaked.

But the black ghast slammed his massive feet to the ground, shaking the earth as he closed in on us. We stumbled, and his huge hand grabbed Natalie around the waist and started crushing her.

She stared at me, eyes bulging in terror.

I found myself hesitating again. I knew she needed help, but I felt heavy and sluggish. I reached inside for a spark of dispelling energy, to sear the black ghast— but instead, I found myself only compelling him to drop Natalie.

He loosened his grip, tossed her aside, and turned his attention to me.

"Emma!" Natalie said, sprawled on the ground. "Stop screwing around and dispel him!"

The ghost roared, and his scalding breath whipped across the playground. I spun away as his spectral fingers plucked at my coat. I held my hands in front of me and fed dispelling energy into them, until in an instant it was crackling between my palms, and I shot the ghost in the side.

He howled and thumped to the ground and started to fade.

That's when the other two ghosts tackled me. I'd stopped compelling them to stay inside the spiderweb.

I yelled at them, *No! Get away from me!* but my panic weakened my compelling. With one on top of me and the other pressing my head into the frozen ground, I watched helplessly as the black ghost stalked toward Natalie. He grabbed her around the waist and flung her into the sandbox.

"No!" I screamed. I dug deep inside for my power, but all I found was that weird humming sound.

Then I heard a voice. "Mind if I cut in?"

I turned and saw two guys stroll onto the playground. The one who spoke was probably my age, dark haired and athletic, wearing a black parka and jeans, and the other was skinny and slightly older, wearing wide-rimmed tortoiseshell glasses and a long camel coat.

The ghosts suffocating me swiveled toward them, their eye sockets burning with predatory intensity. I'd never seen either of these men before in my life, but I was sure of one thing: they were ghostkeepers. And the ghasts felt it, too.

The ghasts' shrieks of fear shook away all my hesitation. I blasted them off me with a burst of force. They hit the ground, scrambled onto all fours like dogs ready to pounce, and rushed at the two newcomers.

The younger guy stepped forward, his arms spread, an eager grin on his face. The ghasts loped closer and closer, then sprang. The young guy used the ghasts' weight and speed against them—he compelled them into the air, over his head, then slammed them onto their backs on top of the slide. Cool trick. As they half skidded down the cold slide, moaning in pain, the older guy shot quick bursts of dispelling energy into them, and they started shimmering into nonexistence.

Martha had taught me basic concepts of ghostkeeping, but no two ghostkeepers were the same. I'd had to figure out myself what worked for me—and it looked nothing like what the ghostkeeper in the glasses had done. Or the other one, for that matter. I'd never realized you could hurl ghosts through the air.

All of that happened in a fraction of a second, while I turned toward the huge black ghast. I drilled through the sluggishness I'd been feeling, to tap my power. He stomped toward me, his face an unearthly mask of fury.

The light inside me grew brighter and hotter until, with the black ghast's unhinged mouth three feet from me, I unleashed a beam of pure white directly into his face. He writhed and shrieked and uncoiled into smoke, which shrank and withered until nothing remained but a smudge of black tar on the wood chips.

The younger guy said, "If this is what you two do at playgrounds, I'd hate to see you in a cemetery."

"Ow," Natalie said, struggling in the sandbox.

"Are you okay?" I asked, jogging over to her.

She took my hand and stood, showing me the ghast-acid holes in her sleeves. "Yeah, but this jacket will never be the same." She looked at the two men. "Who *are* you guys?"

"We're your new team," the one in glasses said, with some kind of accent, maybe English or Irish.

"Looks like we got here just in time," the younger one said. Then he blew on his fingertips and shoved his hands in his pockets, as if he were blowing smoke off the barrels of guns and holstering them.

I knew if I caught Natalie's eye, we'd both burst out giggling. So I just said, "Yeah. Thanks. I'm Emma. The moth-eaten one is Natalie."

"I'm Simon," the older guy said, as he collected the black tar into what looked like a ziplock. "That's Lukas. We'll save the complete introductions until later. Let's get back to the museum."

"One sec," I said. I knelt beside the mound of freshly erupted earth under the tire swing and started digging through the loose dirt.

"If you're looking for the sandbox," Lukas said, "you're like thirty feet off."

"You're desecrating a grave," Simon said. "We don't do that, even if they were ghosts."

"No?" I groped in the oddly warm earth up to my elbow, and suppressed a shiver. I found nothing. Damn. This is where the ghost had come from; shouldn't the dagger be here?

Simon kept scolding me, but I ignored him, too busy concentrating to explain what I was doing. I closed my eyes, opening myself to all the spirits resting fitfully in their graves. This didn't feel like the cemetery where Coby was buried; it felt fragile and dangerous, like ice that was cracking underfoot. I probed the darkness, feeling the restless ache of uneasy ghosts, searching for some sign of the earlier Emma. I'd lived her memories often enough that I'd know when she'd touched something.

I sent tendrils of energy through the playground, and felt an answering warmth. The resonance of Emma's soul.

My eyes flashed open. "It's there."

"What is?" Lukas asked.

"You were right about the sandbox," I told him. Good thing, too, because I hadn't brought a shovel.

I found a plastic bucket in the sand and used it to dig. After I'd made a mound of sand, I tossed the bucket aside and reached down with my hand. I groped in the damp earth until my fingers touched something hard and smooth. Felt like . . . bone. Ick. I suppressed a shiver and kept digging.

Finally I found it, the cold touch of metal. I got a grip and yanked, and pulled the dagger from the earth. It was a long double-edged knife with a hand-forged steel blade and unembellished hilt, except for some intricacy carved into the silver pommel.

"What is that?" Simon demanded.

"Jeez," Lukas said. "The kids play rough around here."

"I'll explain later," I said, tucking it into my coat. "Let's go home."

We shed our coats in the foyer of the museum. Celeste materialized when we came in, and Lukas compelled her to hang our stuff in the hall closet—which bugged me. It's not like she wouldn't have done it anyway, and it was presumptuous of him to come in and start ordering the ghosts around.

I frowned, but didn't say anything. If he was on the team the Knell had organized, I should try to get along with him. My goal was to catch Neos, and if a team would help with that, I'd let personality conflicts slide.

We went into the dining room, where Anatole had set out chicken sandwiches with the crusts cut off and tea in a silver urn. I laid the dagger on the long mahogany table, crossed to the massive fireplace, and downed a cup of chamomile, feeling the heat of the liquid glide through my body.

I helped myself to a second cup and a sandwich and went to stare at the dagger beside Simon.

"Why did you take this?" he asked. His glasses were slightly steamed from the heat of his tea, and he appeared older than he had at first. Probably in his late twenties. He had small gray eyes and wispy pale-colored hair, not quite blond or brown.

"Where are you from?" I asked, ignoring his question.

"Cambridge. Well, at least recently. I was born in Coventry."

"So, England?"

"Yes, England." To my surprise, he smiled. "I forget there's a Cambridge here."

"And you?" I asked, turning to Lukas, where he was making Natalie giggle by the fire. He was undeniably hot, with a swimmer's build, dark hair, and slightly Asian eyes.

"Boston, born and bred." He crossed his arms. "So you're the famous Emma Vaile."

"She's more notorious," Natalie said. "Even though she completely dropped the ball tonight."

"Um," I said, hanging my head. "Sorry?"

"What do you mean, she dropped the ball?" Lukas said. "She took down that big ugly pretty well."

"After like ten minutes. She could hardly handle those two weenie ghasts."

"Natalie," Simon said. "Many ghostkeepers cannot handle a single ghast."

"I know; I'm one of them! Why do you think I hang with Emma?" She shot me a quick grin. "You guys have barely seen her in action. That should've been a cakewalk. She's not like any other ghostkeeper. She messed up tonight, that's all. Ask her."

I nodded. "She's right. I just—couldn't concentrate."

"We all have off days," Simon said. "Now, back to this knife. How did you know it was there? Why did you want it?"

"What is this?" Lukas asked. "The English Inquisition?"

"No." Simon frowned. "It's a guardian questioning his ward about a lethal weapon."

"Wait, are you in charge of us?" Natalie asked.

Simon set down his tea. "Sadly, yes."

"You're only like ten years older than we are," Lukas said.

Simon sighed. "It's not as though I wanted this job. When William phoned, I didn't precisely jump at the chance to be the guardian of three wayward teenagers."

I turned to Natalie. "Did he just call us wayward?"

She eyed Lukas. "He clearly meant Lukas."

Lukas shot her a cocky smile that looked like the definition of *wayward*.

"Nevertheless," Simon continued, "I am in charge of you, and this team." But he must've decided he wouldn't get anything further from me, because he simply said, "It's late, and you all have school tomorrow. Time for bed."

"You should show Lukas one of the empty rooms," I told Natalie.

"That's all right," he said. "I already compelled the maid to get our rooms ready."

"Well, make sure you lock your door," Natalie said, "before you face the wrath of Emma."

He frowned. "What did I do?"

"Compelled the house ghosts instead of politely . . ." Her voice faded as they stepped into the hall.

I slunk after them, but Simon stopped me. "Emma, a word."

I sighed. So close to making my escape.

"Tell me more about the dagger," Simon said. We both stared at it, lying innocently on the dining room table. "How did you know it was there?"

I glanced into my empty teacup to avoid Simon's gaze. "Edmund, a ghost at school, told me." I sensed he'd see through the lie, but just because he was my guardian didn't mean I had to give up all my secrets.

"And who did it belong to?"

"It was Emma's. She was the one who lived—"

He nodded. "The Knell briefed me."

"Well, there was a group of men who hated her. They used this to bait a trap."

"The one you sprang tonight." He lifted the dagger and turned it over in his hands. "Do you know what this is?"

"Um. A knife? Is that a trick question?"

"Do you know how to use it?"

I felt my right hand clench. "Try me."

He almost smiled. "I rather think I won't. But this isn't merely a dagger." He pushed it across the table to me. "I'm almost certain that Emma imbued this with her power."

"But I didn't notice anything when I picked it up."

"Try it again."

I took the dagger by the hilt. It was well balanced, with a razor-sharp edge despite being buried for hundreds of years. Didn't feel like anything special. I shook my head at Simon, but he told me to give it more time. So I closed my eyes and probed further, accustoming myself to the weight of it in my hand and the fine dents in the silver pommel. I ran my thumb over the guard, and that's when I experienced that familiar spinning, like being on a merry-go-round, with that great whooshing sound.

When I opened my eyes, I stood in a cornfield, under a night sky filled with an impossible number of stars. My heart raced and my breath came fast. It was one of Emma's memories, but I experienced it as though it were happening to me right now.

Her heavy skirts whirled around my ankles, her white linen blouse stuck to my back with sweat. Not a great sensation, but it paled in comparison to *her* terror that *I* was experiencing. In my right hand I gripped the hilt of her dagger.

Behind me, a big bearded man stalked through the

rows of corn. I saw his face in the starlight and recognized the features, even though I'd only ever seen him distorted by death and the Beyond. He was the black ghast. Only still alive.

He disappeared into the swaying corn and taunted me in a low, malicious whisper. I spun, feeling Emma's terror and her iron determination. Hunching low, I slipped toward the distant light of a farmhouse.

The man's voice grew fainter as I ran faster. Then he burst from a row in front of me, a cudgel in his hand. As the other Emma, I didn't hesitate. Instead of turning and running, as he clearly expected, I lunged at him. The dagger caught him in the stomach. I pulled my arm back and stabbed him in the chest, blind with fear and fury and loathing.

Inside her body, feeling what she felt, I wanted her to stop. But I couldn't control the memory. Couldn't stop my arm from slashing, not until I heard footsteps behind me. Another man. I fled, leaving the knife behind me, caught in the big man's chest.

The rows of corn whipped past in a blur—spinning, spinning until with a *whoosh,* the dining room reappeared around me.

And I found myself sobbing in Simon's arms on the floor.

"It's okay," he said. "You're here, you're safe."

"She stabbed that man. That ghast. She stabbed him over and over. And I felt like it was me, that I did it." Tears streamed down my cheeks. "He wasn't a ghost—he was alive, and she killed him. I think—I think she lost control. What if I—"

"I'll help you with that," Simon said. "With control."

"I can't use the dagger." I shivered. "Every time I touch it, I'll remember."

"You'll learn to control that, too. To decide how much you want to remember, and when. I don't know half as much as Yoshiro, but I know enough to help. Why do you think William called me?" He nodded toward the door. "It wasn't to keep those two in line; it was to help you."

I stared at the dagger that I'd dropped onto the floor. I was drawn to it, in a way that frightened me. And I didn't know if it was the lingering memories of Emma's, or my own desires.

Simon helped me to my feet. "You should get some sleep." He waited until I was at the door before saying, "Oh, and Emma?"

"Yes?"

"The ghost Edmund didn't tell you about that dagger. I'd prefer if you didn't lie to me."

I nodded briefly, went upstairs, and locked myself in my room. I stared at my homework but thought about the memory of killing the man in the cornfields.

I wasn't just seeing and talking to ghosts anymore. The wraiths at the Knell, the ghasts at the playground. It was all life and death. When had things changed? I used to argue with Bennett about dispelling ghosts, yet I was the one doing most of the killing these days. I pictured the Emma in the tapestry at the Knell. She hadn't looked afraid. She looked as though she liked slaying ghosts. And now I knew my Emma had turned into someone who could kill a man, not just a ghost. I worried that it was going to take that kind of fierce darkness to finish Neos, and that it wasn't a place I wanted to be.

8

I kept my head down during school the next day, and things seemed slightly better. Like I'd moved from a living hell to mere purgatory. Either Natalie's speech had succeeded, or I was getting major points for introducing a new cute guy to school. Anyway, there were fewer frowns and more nods than the day before. Even from some of the girls, who tended to be less forgiving than boys.

Kylee caught me just inside the front hall and offered to pair up with me for fencing. Kylee was ninety pounds soaking wet, and could barely lift her own backpack, yet still could kick my ass at fencing. She was good at following the intricate rules. I was good at killing wraiths, not executing perfect coupés.

"I noticed you and Sara are kind of . . ." She tilted her head, waiting for me to finish.

"Yeah," I said, unwilling to go into details. Everyone knew Sara and Coby were best friends. How hard was it to figure out why we'd stopped talking to each other?

"Anyway," she said, "I promise to go easy on you."

"Thanks," I said, heading off to Latin. I knew there was a reason I'd always been nice to her, despite the butt-kickings.

Natalie was across the room leaning on Harry's desk, seemingly flirting with him. The traitor. I went and sat next to Lukas, who sprawled at a desk that he made look miniature. He was even taller than I'd realized.

"I think I'm in love," Lukas said.

"With who? You've only been here like ten minutes."

"Okay, so it's lust."

I glanced at him in alarm. "Not with Natalie."

He sat up straighter. "What? She's hot. Though I'd have to be a fool to fall for another ghostkeeper."

I grunted.

"Oh, sorry. Forgot about you and Bennett."

Natalie sauntered over to join us. "Did you tell him about Bennett?" I asked.

"It's no secret, Emma," she said. "You're like a legend in the ghostkeeping world. Word gets around."

Great. My heartbreak the subject of Knell gossip. Just what I needed.

"What were you doing talking to Harry?" I asked.

"Intel," she said. "Trying to figure out how to end this feud between you."

"And?" I asked, hoping for some inspiration.

"And he smelled like booze."

"Already?" I glanced at him and he glared back at me.

"That's not good," Lukas said in Latin. The dead

language came easily to him. He was a ghostkeeper. We bring the dead to life.

Lukas sat with me and Natalie for lunch. He swaggered in, looking edgy and sexy in his uniform. I swear I heard girls sigh as he passed their tables. Harry and Sara were conspicuously absent, which was a relief. Though I wondered if Harry was off drinking and if Sara had joined him, just like she used to down espressos with him.

I still needed to talk to them about Coby. Add that to my list of impossible things I needed to accomplish.

Lukas seemed oblivious to the effect he had as he dug into his lunch. I noticed Anatole had packed Lukas what he must've considered a "man's meal." While Natalie and I were given fruit salad and whole-grain rolls, Lukas had a thick ham sandwich and potato chips. Then I wondered if he'd compelled Anatole to make that.

I was about to ask when he said, "Wow. Who's *she*?"

We looked up and saw Britta. She was in my Trig and Western Civ classes, and we hated each other. Though, I had to admit, she was pretty, with long tawny hair and peachy skin. She was one of those girls who's curvy yet minuscule at the same time. And no, that's not why I hated her.

Lukas smiled, and Britta flashed her fangs at him.

"You're new, right?" she cooed. "I think you're sitting at the wrong table."

"Yeah?"

"Mm-hmm. Because mine is over *there*." She gave him a coy look. "And I'd love to show you *everything*."

Lukas nodded slowly, like he was considering, and I held my breath. Britta was easy and hot, and he was a guy. But he just took another bite of his sandwich. "Nah, I'm good."

Britta's face flushed, and she turned on her heel and marched back to her table.

"Why didn't you go with her?" Natalie asked. "She's cute. Chock full of nuts, but cute."

"We've got girls like that in Boston," he said. "Fake as her nails."

I hadn't been sure about Lukas, because of the whole compelling-the-house-ghosts thing, but at least he was a good judge of character. It was a relief to think I might have another friend around here.

After school, the three of us met at the gate and walked back to the museum together. Lukas amused us with stories of life at his old school in Boston, two hundred years old and packed with resident ghosts. Lukas had been the only ghostkeeper, but he couldn't summon, so he had to wait for them to appear on their own. When they did, he'd compel them to play pranks on teachers and kids who bugged him. The students and faculty had started saying the place was haunted when the Knell finally contacted him.

As we walked down the long gravel drive through the

stand of maple trees, I begged Lukas not to start that game at Thatcher. I had enough problems.

"Actually," Natalie said thoughtfully, "he won't have to wait for them. I'll summon them, then he'll compel them."

"Natalie!"

"What? It's funny."

The two of them spent the rest of the walk home plotting pranks, as I loftily ignored them.

When we opened the front door, Simon stood in the foyer, waiting for us.

"There is a snack waiting in the kitchen," he said.

"I'm not hungry," Natalie said. "I'm going for a run."

She started up the stairs, but Simon's voice stopped her in her tracks. "Natalie, you may change your clothes, then you will join Emma and Lukas for sustenance in the kitchen."

Sustenance? Who uses words like sustenance?

"Then you will all meet me in the ballroom," Simon continued. "Yes, we dispelled a handful of ghasts, but next we face wraiths. And then Neos. He's killed six ghostkeepers already—I'd prefer if none of you were number seven."

Natalie glanced at me, as though waiting for a protest. I shrugged. "We could use the practice."

She turned to Lukas. He said, "I could eat again."

Natalie rolled her eyes. "I already know how to summon. What is there for me to practice?"

"Returning them," Simon said.

"You mean dispelling them?" Lukas asked. "She can't do that; she's a summoner."

"Dispellers send spirits to their mortal form, dead in the ground. However, summoners can learn to return ghosts they've summoned back into the Beyond."

"What?" Natalie said. "No, we can't."

"You can if you're taught properly."

"Why didn't anyone ever tell me that?" Natalie asked, hand on one hip.

"Because you never met me before. It's an old art, and rarely used, as we always team a dispeller with a summoner. But it's possible."

"Where'd you learn this stuff?" I asked.

"From Yoshiro," he said. "And far too many dusty books. Now go change; your snack's waiting in the kitchen."

We headed upstairs, and Natalie said, "Do you think he's all talk?"

"I don't know. Maybe it sounds believable because of his accent. We'll find out soon enough."

I shucked my uniform and sank into gray yoga pants and a black tank top. If Simon's drills were anything like Martha's, I knew I'd be sweating, but in the meantime I tossed on a red cashmere hoodie that belonged to my mom. I hadn't taken it to the cleaners and it still smelled a little of her perfume. Maybe my mom and I didn't have the best relationship, but I still missed her. With each passing day, I began to worry that something really terrible had happened to her and my dad and Max. The longer I didn't hear from them, the more I thought I never would. They were all ghostkeepers. If they were dead, they were dead. No ghosts lingering in the Beyond.

When I met Natalie in the hall, she was dressed in her running gear. "You're not—"

She shrugged. "It's comfortable. Besides, this can't take all afternoon."

We met Lukas in the kitchen. He'd changed into jeans and a white T-shirt and sat happily sipping soup from a little Chinese bowl.

I looked closer and saw brown rice. I peered at Anatole. *Is that . . . miso?*

Do not even say that word! Mi-so. His mustache bristled. *This is not soup; this is an offense against God and man.*

But . . . where are the cakes and cookies? The berries and homemade lemonade? There was a solarium off the kitchen, like a fancy greenhouse where Anatole grew orange and lemon trees.

Don't look to me, chéri. It is that horrible pale fellow, Simon. This was hiz doing.

But how did he ask you?

He pointed to a note, sitting on the kitchen counter. There were detailed instructions about how long to cook the rice and prepare the miso.

You can read? I asked.

Anatole scoffed. *But of course. And in any case,* we *can oftentimes understand* you. *It iz just the living who cannot understand the dead. Unless you are a communicator, that iz to say. Then you ask the insulting questions—if I can read!*

I'm sorry. It's just I've read in old books that servants—

I am no servant! His French accent was even thicker than usual, which meant I'd really upset him. *Pah. You are young. But have a talk with zat . . . horrible fellow. Hiz cooking iz not for me.*

I nodded, chastised, and sipped my miso. It was surprisingly tasty.

Fifteen minutes later, we all shuffled into the ballroom, where Simon was waiting. He wore a gray tracksuit and a whistle around his neck.

"Let's begin," he said.

"Sure, Coach," Lukas said. "Should we run laps?"

Natalie clapped. "Yeah, we've gotta get ready for the Big Game."

Simon blew his whistle. "Lukas, shut up. Natalie, summon a ghost from the harbor."

"What?" she said. "I can't, that's way too far."

"That's the first lesson—the rules are changing. Nobody has more than one ability, right? We all learned that. Except Emma has *all* the abilities. Possession is impossible, right? Not any more. Nobody's seen a wraith in centuries—but Neos is creating an army of them, right now. We're living through some big, scary changes. You don't know what's possible. You don't know the extent of your powers."

"And you do?" Natalie asked.

"Not always," he said. "But I know that the old rules don't apply. And I've spent enough time reading myths and legends to push you in the right direction. Close your eyes, Natalie. Concentrate. Picture the harbor. Imagine you're there, smell the air, feel the breeze. Then open yourself to the lingering spirits . . ."

His voice turned to an almost hypnotic drone as he murmured to her, guiding her through an unseen maze of spectral powers. He worked with her for several minutes, while Lukas and I lounged on the floor and gossiped about school.

"So, is Thatcher anything like your old school?" I asked.

"Nah." Lukas glanced toward the ceiling, thinking about it. "I never thought I'd say this, but I sort of miss the thugs."

"I know, right? The scariest thing about Thatcher is the uniforms."

"What do you think you're doing?" Simon towered over us.

"Uh, waiting for Natalie to summon a ghost?" Lukas said.

"You think her lesson doesn't apply to you? That these techniques won't help you become a better compeller? She's broadening her mind, and you're chatting like magpies. She's your teammate; give her a little respect. And *you*"—he turned his full disgust on me—"I expected better. You can summon; you need to master *all* these lessons."

We watched in chastened silence while Natalie summoned ghosts from the harbor, a gnarled old sea dog, then a woman with feathered seventies hair. Then it was my turn. I summoned a zitty teenager, and Lukas and I practiced compelling all three of them—though I insisted on asking permission first. Simon said we could use them to fight wraiths. I wasn't sure how I felt about using innocent ghosts against wraiths, especially as they weren't as strong or as flesh-hungry as wraiths, but Simon didn't have any time for my second thoughts.

He barked at me like a drill sergeant—this wasn't about me and my dainty concerns, he said, this was about stopping Neos before he rose to his full power in the realm of the living. Simon was brutal. Despite his bony body and horn-rimmed glasses, he drove us mercilessly.

By six o'clock, we were zonked, dining miserably on tofu steaks and grilled vegetables in the dining room. Part of the training regimen. And for the record, Limoges china and antique silver did not make this palatable.

During the next week, we fell into an exhausting routine. School, training, Buddhist monastery food, then school and training again. One evening, I woke in the middle of the night to a tingling in my fingers. I blinked away the scattered memories of a dream: the beautiful woman with short dark hair, wide eyes, and red lipstick, whispering in my ear. Lovely words that made me feel safe.

When the tingling in my hand turned to burning, I

came fully awake, and saw a ghost at the edge of my bed, clutching my hand. Not the short-haired woman, but a long-haired Latina girl with a sad face.

Panicked, I pulled away, and the ghost put a finger to her mouth. *Shhh. Your brother sent me.*

I stopped reaching for the power inside me. *Who are you?* I asked.

That doesn't matter. She drifted a little higher. *Your brother, Max, compelled me to memorize a message for you.*

That's not even possible, sending ghost messages.

Your brother found a way. There are new ways all the time.

Just like Simon had said, the old rules no longer applied. *How do I know this isn't some ploy of Neos's?*

There is a hostile spirit near, the ghost said. *But not me. I am compelled to deliver this message. Then you will not see me again.*

What's wrong with texting? I asked. *The phone, e-mail . . .*

A wave of luminescence washed over her. *This is the message.*

Wait—how did he communicate with you? How'd he find me? How do I find him?

But the ghost wasn't listening. Instead, she spoke in Max's voice: *I wasn't involved with the ghostkeeper killings, Em. I hope you believe that. Neither were Mom and Dad. We're trying to defeat Neos, and we don't trust the Knell. You need to find Neos's resting place, where his body is buried. Maybe then you can defeat him. Maybe.*

Maybe? What am I supposed to do once I find the—

The ghost message spoke right over me: *He's absorbing*

power from Mom's amulet, and once he masters that, he'll mas-
ter possession. But we think he needs to perform some final rite.
He's afraid to confront you, though, so he's trying to weaken
you first. We think he summoned a—

She stopped, shimmering in the darkness.

"A what?" I said aloud.

We think he summoned a—

"C'mon! Summoned a *what*? Are you skipping? You're
not a CD. And what do I do once I find his final resting place?"

—think he summoned— The ghost girl grabbed herself
around the throat and started squeezing. *—summoned a—*

Stop! Stop doing that!

I compelled her to stop, but my powers felt weak and
dim, and she kept squeezing until her face grew mottled,
her eyes bulged in pain, but I couldn't save her.

A siren, she gasped, and faded away.

I sat there in bed, my hand covering my mouth like
some shocked Victorian lady, my heart pounding. After a
while, I leaned back against the headboard and thought
for a long time about Rachel and her warning about a
siren. What could that mean? Could it be worse than
a wraith? Impossible. And the poor ghost Max had sent—
was she dead?

Then my stomach growled and I stopped thinking. I
pulled on my wool sweater and some socks and padded
downstairs into the kitchen, hoping for something other
than a crust of millet bread.

I found Anatole putting the finishing touches on an

ice cream sundae in a fluted bowl, with Celeste setting one place at the table and Nicholas watching me with a boyish grin. With a slight bow, Anatole handed me the bowl with a silver dessert spoon.

You are a god. I was in heaven from the first spoonful. I bet he made the sauce himself. *How did you know I was coming?*

Nicholas heard you wake. And how could you not be hungry after that shameful meal theez evening?

You don't have to do what he says, you know.

Celeste shrugged. *Iz our duty.*

Lukas must be starving, I said, savoring the vanilla ice cream.

Non, Anatole said. *He was here not an hour ago, compelling me to make him a zandwich.*

And me to run the shower for him afterward, Celeste said.

He made me trot like a horse in circles around his room, Nicholas grumbled.

He'll regret that, I fumed. *He's gotten away with way too much.*

The ghosts smiled in relief and we chatted for a while. I asked them if they knew what a siren was. Anatole had heard of the Greek myth, but Nicholas thought I was talking about the sound on a fire truck. Not at all helpful.

I finished my sundae, and Celeste sent Nicholas to stoke the fire in my room. As I nestled back under the covers, the fear and confusion of the night had mellowed into something warm. The ghosts were a surrogate family to me, always ready with a kind word and dessert. As bad as things got, I needed to remember all the good things, too. Like the fact that I was too busy to miss Bennett.

Okay, that wasn't a good thing. That was just a lie. If he were here, we could've eaten sundaes in the kitchen together. I thought about the little ice cream stand he'd promised to take me to. Memorial Day seemed awfully far away. I wondered what Bennett's favorite flavor was. I wanted to know everything about him, like if he always got rum raisin.

9

The next day at school, Lukas caught up with me in the hallway. "Do you know her?"

He nodded toward Sara, wandering aimlessly through the halls, looking like . . . well, like someone just killed her best friend. Sara normally appeared ready for the paparazzi, even in her uniform. Perfect hair, killer shoes, envy-worthy bag. Today her hair looked like something had nested in it. And, my God, were those sneakers on her feet?

"I did," I said, still baffled about how I could make everything good between us.

"She looks sad," he said.

"She was in love with Coby."

"Maybe she just needs someone new to get him off her mind." He glanced at her, appraisingly.

"Leave her alone," I said, sharply. "And while we're on the subject . . ."

"What did I do?"

He tried to appear innocent, but failed, and I gave him an earful about treating the ghosts in the museum better.

"They're only ghosts," he said.

Could he really be so dense? "No," I said, "they're people, even if they are dead. And if I find out you've made Nicholas trot around like a horse again—"

He towered over me, a slight grin on his face. In my tirade, I'd forgotten how tall he was. "You'll what, Emma?"

The class bell rang, and I didn't have time to come up with a better threat than, "You don't want to find out."

Then I marched away, before he could mock me.

I sprawled next to Natalie on the gym floor, waiting for Fencing to start.

"Have you seen Coby?" I asked. I hadn't seen him since I sent him off with Edmund.

"No." She pulled her hair back and started to braid it. "Why?"

"I don't know," I said. "I'm just worried about him."

Natalie glanced at the two ghost jocks sitting in the stands. "It can't be easy, turning into a ghost."

"No," I agreed. "Especially if you get bossed around by some loose-cannon compeller."

"You still pissed at Lukas?" She snapped a hair band around the base of her braid.

"I talked to him, but I don't think he took me seriously."

"I don't think he takes anything seriously."

We stood as Coach came in, and my helmet, which I'd propped on my head like sunglasses, slipped and clattered to the wooden floor.

The ghost jocks snorted, and one said, *And they say she can kill wraiths.*

Sure, if she trips and falls on them, the other said. Then they laughed hysterically. It was like having my own personal booing team.

"You have to admit he's cute, though," Natalie said, handing me back my helmet. "Think one of his parents is Asian?"

"I don't know. Didn't you ask?" It wasn't like Natalie was shy.

"He doesn't talk about his parents much," she mused, a dreamy look in her eyes. "It's hard to believe that gorgeous face could be the product of two boring white people."

He was undeniably hot, even if I was in love with someone else. But Natalie's dazed look said something more. "You like him, don't you?"

"What?" she said. "With Harry gone, there's no one worth flirting with, that's all."

"Fine." Who was I to deny Natalie a little innocent flirtation? God knows what kind of trouble she'd get into without it.

After lunch, I found a quiet corner in the library and tried to sense Coby and Edmund. I didn't immediately feel either of them, and didn't push it. After yelling at Lukas for bossing ghosts around, it seemed hypocritical to summon them. Instead I researched my World Civ paper.

The rest of the day went okay—still a little chilly, socially, but Harry was gone and I managed to avoid Sara. Lukas was too busy flirting with a senior girl to join us at the gate, so Natalie and I walked home together.

We talked about nothing in particular until I suddenly blurted, "Max contacted me."

She frowned. "How?"

"By ghost," I said. "He compelled some girl to memorize a message and sent her to me."

"I've never heard of that."

"Me either. Wonder if Simon has. Anyway, she . . ." I started to explain more about the ghost girl, but a familiar humming noise suddenly filled my brain.

"She what?" Natalie asked.

"What?" I tried to clear my head. "I don't know. I forgot what I was going to say."

"Is Max all right?"

"He's okay, I guess. I got the sense he wasn't in Nepal or Tibet—wherever he's supposed to be. He said he didn't have anything to do with the ghostkeeper killings, thank you, Captain Obvious. And then there was some stuff about defeating Neos." I bit my lip. "Do you think that's what he's been doing all along—looking for Neos? Did he know before we did that Neos was responsible? Why wouldn't he tell the Knell?"

Natalie shrugged. "Your parents aren't really fans."

"Mmm. Do you think I should tell Simon?"

"Why wouldn't you?"

"I don't know. What if Max has a legitimate reason for keeping this stuff from the Knell?" I'd tell Bennett, even though he'd probably spill it to the Knell, but he wasn't here.

Natalie fiddled with her hair, looking like she wasn't sure if she wanted to say something.

"What?" I asked.

"Nothing. I—I heard from Bennett. He texted me to make sure we're okay. I guess he heard about the ghasts."

I stopped on the sidewalk. "Where is he?"

"He didn't say."

Why had he texted her and not me? It made me sick to my stomach. It was okay when I thought he was ignoring both of us, but now it felt like his friendship with Natalie was more important that whatever was going on between him and me.

"Did he mention me?" I felt pathetic asking, but had to know.

"He wanted to make sure you're okay."

"Then why didn't he text *me*?" I kicked a pile of fallen maple leaves. "Guys are so confusing. All girls want is to know where we stand. He and I have this perfect night in New York, and the next morning he's barely speaking to me. Now he can't even bother to text me? Guys are supposed to be the straightforward communicators, but they're not. They have no idea how they feel, what they should say or not say. They suck. And it's not just that they suck, they—"

"Emma!"

I realized she'd said my name three times. "What?"

"Bennett loves you. You know that. You just have to wait until we dispel Neos. Then you can ride off into the sunset together or whatever."

I grunted. "I guess. But guys still suck."

"Don't talk that way," Lukas said, stepping beside me. "You're hurting my feelings."

"You're an idiot," Natalie told him.

"Are you saying that just because I'm a guy?" Lukas asked.

Natalie shrugged, as if to say, what more reason did she need?

"Then I guess that makes you a girl who likes idiots," he said.

She gave him that coy smile she does so well. "What makes you say that?"

I felt like a third wheel as they continued teasing each other the rest of the way home. I tried to tune them out, torn between hating Bennett for not contacting me and wishing he were here so I could do a little flirting myself.

After suffering through yet another soy-based dinner, I found Simon in Bennett's father's office. He'd trained us so hard that afternoon that we'd saluted and called him Sarge. Sitting on the little sofa, reading a book bound in gray leather, he didn't look any worse for wear. He bookmarked his place when I came in, and the soft light of the lamp reflected off his glasses, making it hard to judge his expression.

"What is it, Emma?"

I stood there in the doorway, unsure where to start.

"Have a seat," he said, gesturing to one near him. "Would you like some chocolate?"

The offer surprised a laugh from me. "Have you *met* me?"

He smiled and handed me a bar of expensive dark chocolate. I broke off a square, popped it in my mouth, and savored the intense flavor as it melted, trying to gather my thoughts. I wanted to tell him everything, but he was still a stranger to me. And from the Knell.

He said, "You don't know if you can trust me."

I stopped chewing. "How did you know?"

"It's only natural, Emma. You've been treated unfairly, kept in the dark for most of your life. But I can't talk you into trusting me. That's a decision you'll have to make for yourself."

"Yeah, I just— I need to talk to someone who knows this stuff." I didn't say anything for a minute, then made a decision. "I heard from Max. My brother. I don't know if you . . ."

He nodded. "He's missing, along with your parents."

I nodded. "At least, now I know he's alive."

"Did he phone? It's possible the Knell could trace his call."

"They can do that?"

He tilted his head. "We have friends in law enforcement."

"Oh," I said. "He sent a ghost."

"Really?" Simon sat straighter, listening intently as I explained. "That's remarkable. I've read of ghostkeepers doing that, but not in quite a long time. I wonder how he learned to do it."

"My dad's library is bigger than this one." I nodded toward the shelves filled with old tomes. "And Max read them all."

"I think I'd enjoy your father's library," he said. "When this is all over, of course."

"When *is* it going to be over?" I asked, praying he had an answer. Simon seemed to be training us for some specific moment, but never said what. Was he waiting for instructions from the Knell? Or for the moment when Neos tried to kill me?

"Let's start with Max," he said. "What did he tell you?"

I told him what the ghost had said about my mother's amulet. I wanted to say more, but I couldn't seem to find the right words. "And . . . um . . . I guess that's it."

Simon didn't say anything for a minute after I finished, his brow furrowed in thought. Then he said, "Let's talk it out. Neos needs some final rite to absorb the power from your mother's amulet. He's afraid of you, and plans to kill you. *And* he summoned a siren to weaken you, so he'll succeed. Is that correct?"

"Yeah. Plus we need to find where Neos is buried, for some reason."

"Perhaps that's a point of vulnerability. No one knows what will happen to Neos when we dispel him."

"So where is he buried?" I asked.

He frowned. "No one knows that, either."

"Then how can we find him?"

He tapped the cover of the gray book. "I suggest we start with the mausoleum where he killed the man for the amulet."

"I don't understand why my mother's amulet gives Neos so much power." He'd used it to steal the powers of other ghostkeepers, by carving its designs into their flesh before he murdered them. And somehow it had allowed him to possess Coby.

"He killed himself over your mother, and a piece of her is tied to that jade amulet. Ghostkeeping isn't a science, Emma. It's magic. And love is another kind of magic—he's bound to her. He also has some of your blood, doesn't he?"

I touched the scar on the inside of my forearm, where Neos had cut me as a child.

"He's bound to you, as well," Simon said. "There are no easy answers, Emma. He's groping in the dark for power, while we stumble around blindly after him."

I let out a sigh. "We really have to go back to the mausoleum?"

"After I finish researching it, yes."

"And what about the siren? I tried looking it up but I didn't find much. I thought I heard a weird humming noise at the playground. Could that have something to do with the siren?"

"A humming noise, huh?" Simon mused. "In Greek mythology the sirens are enchantresses, bird-women who lived on these islands called Sirenum scopuli. They lured sailors to their deaths with songs of irresistible beauty."

"If you tell me we're fighting a bunch of Greek myths, I am going to scream."

He half laughed. "That's just the origin. There are whispers of a creature in the Beyond with the same power, but she's a myth, just like the bird-women. The humming is probably just due to stress. I'm more concerned about finding Neos's final resting spot. I'm not aware of any connection between him and any burial ground other than that mausoleum."

We talked for a while about Neos. Then Simon launched into a lecture about his theory of ghasts—which wasn't even all that boring. He'd make a good professor someday. Then he stopped and looked at me. "May I see your ring?"

I hesitated a moment before pulling the chain from inside my shirt.

Simon reached a finger out tentatively and touched the ring. Then he shook his head. "I can't feel any power. Does it really turn you into a ghost?"

I nodded. "But I don't like using it much."

"It's embedded with the other Emma's powers. It's not unlike the dagger. How is your training going?"

"You know better than anyone—you just spent three hours kicking my butt."

"I mean, with the dagger."

"Um. You wanna spar?"

"Not me," he said. "Your . . . friend."

"Oh." He knew about the Rake. "I haven't shown it to him yet."

"Well, you should. Learn to use it before your life depends on it. Before all our lives depend on it."

Upstairs in my bedroom, I pulled Emma's dagger from the drawer, where it was buried under my T-shirts. The hilt felt cold and heavy, and I almost hid it away immediately. I didn't want to face this—another weapon, more killing.

But no matter how scared I was of Neos, or worried that I'd inevitably become cold-blooded, like that Emma in the tapestry, I had to do this. There was no one else who could finish Neos, no one strong enough to protect Natalie and the others, and avenge Martha's and Coby's deaths. And it was the only way Bennett and I could ever be together.

So I grabbed the dagger and wandered downstairs. I stood quietly in the center of the ballroom, not bothering to summon the Rake. I knew the power in Emma's dagger would draw him. It only took a moment for him to materialize. He strode across the parquet floor, looking pleased to see me. Then his expression changed.

Oh, my dear child, he said, with such emotion that tears sprang to my eyes. I didn't expect sympathy from *him*.

I'm okay, I said. Though I wasn't. *I'm just ready for a vacation, a few days to pretend I'm an ordinary girl.*

I wish I could fight him for you, Emma. But you're the only one who's strong enough.

I know. I just wish the Knell took care of this, instead of getting their asses kicked. Why can't they just dispatch some assassin to track down Neos?

His eyebrow arched mockingly, but his expression remained kind.

And I realized: *Oh. They think* I'm *their assassin.* I showed the Rake the dagger. *In that case, I definitely need you to teach me how to use this.*

Any problems retrieving it?

The ghasts were meaner than I expected, I said. *And I kind of froze up.*

That happens. You're young.

I guess. I looked at the dagger's lethal blade. *And later, when I grabbed the knife, I flashed on Emma's memory of killing a man. I mean, a living man. She was vicious. I don't want to be like—*

She was fighting for her life, he said.

I know, but—

You would do the same. You must *do the same. Your qualms speak well of you—but you are not simply an ordinary girl. You are Emma Vaile. Never forget that.*

Yeah, like anyone's gonna let me forg—

He slashed at me with his rapier, and I jerked backward, raising the dagger to ward off the blow.

Would you stop doing that? I said.

Your grip is wrong.

That's how Emma held it, I told him.

You're stronger than she was, and quicker. She was good with a dagger, but she could never best me.

Neither have I, I said glumly.

But you will. Hold it like this.

Wait. You think I can beat you? Tell me more. I like that idea.

He shot me a look. *If you can't beat me, you can't beat Neos. And you* will *beat Neos. So try this.* He moved my hand into a different position, and I tried not to wince as the touch of his fingers burned my own. *And remember, it's not a sword.*

He showed me how to slash and thrust, to feint and wrestle with my off-hand. We spent an hour on deflecting blows and counterattacking. I didn't see how a dagger could ever stand against a sword, but the Rake ignored my complaints and just attacked me again. He explained I needed to get close and up-cut through the heart of a wraith, or through the empty eye sockets.

He didn't let me stop until I managed to slam him in the temple with the dagger's hilt in a quick reverse.

Well done, the Rake said, rubbing his head.

That's the nicest thing you've ever said to me. I licked the blood from a cut on my hand. *But I still don't see how a dagger's better than a sword.*

When you fight in earnest, you'll infuse the blade with your powers, he said. *Stay safe.* He faded out.

Upstairs, I bandaged the cut on my hand, wondering if the Rake knew that he'd echoed the last words Bennett had said to me. Not for the first time, I pondered how much our lives were a replay of what came before. And what did that mean for me and Bennett? Would he lose his ghostkeeping abilities, or were we destined to remain apart forever?

10

A few days passed, again filled with nothing but school, training, a macrobiotic diet, and homework. Then one afternoon, Simon greeted us at the door of the museum. "Change of plans," he said. "Dress warmly."

We shuffled upstairs to slip into wool socks and fleeces, then back downstairs into the kitchen to gulp green tea and chew trail mix, as Anatole looked on in dismay. Celeste attempted to soothe his offended sense of propriety, while Nicholas grinned at me over his Game Boy.

Lukas said, "Hey, ask the kid if I can have a turn."

I blinked at him. "Why don't you just compel him?"

"Because you'll yell at me again."

I asked Nicholas to share.

"Plus," Natalie said, "I told him if he keeps being rude, I'll tell everyone at school that the two of you are secretly dating. He'd be an outcast in like three seconds."

Lukas snorted, accepting the Game Boy from Nicholas.

"Gee, thanks," I told Natalie.

"No problem."

Simon called from the front hall. We found him waiting at the door, dressed in an olive turtleneck and his long camel coat. He greeted us by saying, "I'm sure Emma's told you about the message from her brother."

Natalie nodded, but Lukas complained. "What? I didn't even know she *had* a brother."

"That's 'cause you're an idiot," Natalie murmured.

"For the last time, I am not an idiot!"

"*Children*," Simon said.

They shut up, and I filled in Lukas about Max sending me a message. "So where are we off to?" I asked, as I shrugged into my black peacoat. "Did you find Neos's burial site?"

"No," Simon answered. "We're on a fact-finding mission."

"Intriguing," Lukas mocked.

As usual, Simon ignored him. "The last time a ghost-keeper visited this place, he was killed by wraiths."

"Really?" Lukas cracked his knuckles. "That's more like it."

"Where?" Natalie asked, frowning. Lukas had never dealt with a wraith before; he was excited at the prospect, but Natalie and I knew better.

"The mausoleum," Simon said.

"What mausoleum?" Lukas asked, handing the Game Boy back to Nicholas, who'd followed us.

I opened the front door. "The place where Neos stole my mother's amulet."

"What amulet?" Lukas asked. "Why do I always feel like I'm missing key pieces of information?"

Natalie grinned. "Because you're an—"

"Don't say it!"

Simon sighed. "Just get in the car, you two."

The car was an electric blue Yaris. Lukas called shotgun, and Natalie and I squeezed into the back while Simon drove.

"Couldn't the Knell afford something better than this?" Natalie asked, her knees pressing into Lukas's seat. "It has that rental-car smell."

"Yeah," Lukas said. "Like old shoes and popcorn."

"Nah. That's movie-theater smell," Natalie said. "This is more like baby wipes and tuna fish."

"Can you imagine if we showed up at school in this thing?" I asked, thinking of Sara's BMW.

"I've seen worse in the parking lot," Lukas said. "There's that junker Focus."

"That doesn't count," I said.

"It belongs to that kid who wears that green tracksuit over his uniform," Natalie explained.

I shifted in my seat, trying to get comfortable. "You ought to flirt with him. He's some kind of computer geek. He'll probably end up one of those tech billionaires."

"Oh, that guy," Lukas said, nodding. "What about the blue Su—"

"Quiet!" Simon snapped. "Don't you children realize where we're going? We're not off to the candy store. We're headed to a cemetery where one of our own was killed.

You should use this time to focus your powers. And if not, have a little reverence for a ghostkeeper who was killed in the line of duty. Get your heads on!"

We were quiet for three miles as we all contemplated Simon's outburst. Then Natalie broke the silence. "You still didn't say why you chose this car."

"It gets good mileage," Simon ground out.

It was four o'clock when we arrived at the cemetery, and shadows were lengthening over the gravestones. The snow that fell on the day of Coby's funeral had melted, but patches of ice lurked in potholes and under drifts of brown leaves. Simon parked, and we crossed the street and stood at the wooden gates. A stone wall surrounded the graveyard, the smallest and oldest in Salem.

"There's a lot of . . ." Natalie didn't finish her sentence. She didn't have to; we all felt the lingering ghosts vying for our attention. Old ghosts were powerful, and some of these had been around for three hundred years.

"Yeah," Lukas said.

"Why are there so many?" I asked Simon.

"It's a nexus, concentrated in this cemetery. That's no doubt why Neos lured the other ghostkeeper here with the amulet. He has a lot of power in a place like this."

"But he doesn't know we're here, right?" Natalie asked, anxiously.

"Of course not," Simon said. "Nobody knew we were coming here until just now. We're perfectly safe."

I almost mentioned that Yoshiro had thought the same about the Knell, but the words stuck in my throat. I tried to comfort Natalie instead. "If it's a nexus, then we're more powerful here, too."

"Right. So this is the plan," Simon said. "I've hit a dead end with my research into Neos's final resting place, and I'm hoping to find a new lead. We're going to question the ghosts. I have a list and a map of the graves. We'll start here and loop around."

"We're going to ask if they know where Neos is buried?" Natalie asked.

Simon nodded. "They probably won't, but they may know about the amulet. Items such as that sometimes leave ripples in the Beyond. Maybe it'll provide a way we can track him."

"They're ghosts," Lukas said. "You really think they'll rat out one of their own?"

"They're not all like that," I said. "You're living with some of the good ones."

Simon led us down the gravel path along the fence. I glanced up at the fading light. "Just once, I'd like to do this at noon."

"Here," Simon said.

Natalie examined the grave. "'Tobias Smith, loving husband and father.'" Then she summoned him. Tobias was a young, stooped man who'd been balding before he died. I relayed Simon's questions to him, and repeated back the unhelpful answers. Then we moved on to the next grave.

An hour and ten summonings later, exhausted and shivering, we'd circled all the way back to the wooden gates without learning anything useful.

"There's one more place to check," Simon said, looking up from his list. "The tomb where the ghostkeeper was murdered."

My mind flashed on a memory of my dream, the poor, pudgy ghostkeeper whose skin had been licked away by wraiths. I glanced toward the tomb in the corner of the cemetery. Made from granite with black iron gates and gargoyle statues, it looked like the place you'd find a vampire.

The others crunched down the path toward the tomb, as I trailed behind. The evening gloom fell around us, and the cemetery felt increasingly *wrong*, the background murmuring of ghosts reaching a high, dissonant pitch.

No one else seemed to notice, but when I stopped to listen, I heard strained whispers though the rustling of the leaves: *Run, hide, they're coming.*

I watched Natalie draw upon her power; I felt the call of her summoning. She closed her eyes and I heard three voices, stronger than the rest, beating in a steady rhythm: *Feed, feed, feed.*

Wraiths.

"Natalie, wait! Stop!"

But I was too late. Natalie unleashed her power, and three wraiths seeped into our world through cracks in the Beyond. Paper-thin skin dangled from their insectoid forms throbbing with hunger and hatred. They were freshly hatched and bloodthirsty and took Natalie, Simon, and Lukas by surprise.

Time slowed. I tried to scream, but I was trapped in fog. The humming was back, blocking out the sound of the ghosts and wraiths. An insistent note, pushing everything else from my mind. Terror rose within me, but then quickly slid away, replaced by a removed sense of calm as the humming began to take on a distinct lullaby-like melody.

As soon as Natalie realized what she'd summoned, she panicked. She scrambled backward and tripped over the edge of the path as a wraith caught her around the neck and scorched her face with its fetid breath.

Simon screamed a few garbled words and shot quick bursts of dispelling energy at the wraith. The wraith screeched and trembled, then turned toward him. Simon's attack wasn't working, but at least Natalie took the opportunity to roll away and summon again. I felt the power radiating from her body, reaching far beyond the cemetery.

I stood watching from a tremendous distance, completely disengaged from my own feelings.

The wraith turned on Simon, and he shot another burst of power that the wraith shrugged off. Lukas was faring better. He used compelling force to channel the speed of an attacking wraith, flipping it over his head and onto a gravestone shaped like a miniature Washington Monument.

The stone impaled the wraith, and it shrieked and

writhed, but refused to die. Instead, it started levitating higher, and Lukas forced it back downward—until he heard Simon shout for help. He turned and saw Simon peppering the other two wraiths with dispelling power, and hardly slowing them as they advanced on him and Natalie.

Lukas compelled the wraiths away from Simon, and they began to slither toward him, ignoring Simon and Natalie.

Natalie gasped at me. "Emma, wake up! They're going to kill Lukas!"

I couldn't move, couldn't push past the humming in my mind.

As the wraiths pushed toward Lukas, the third wraith—now freed from the impaling monument—jumped him from behind and slashed with serrated teeth at his neck. Lukas dropped to one knee and threw the wraith past him—then he staggered, clutching the back of his neck, blood seeping through his fingers. He barely managed to stay on his feet, facing all three wraiths as they came toward him. A clawed hand swept forward to slash his face, as a blur of gray sprang from nowhere and tackled the wraith.

It was Coby! That's who Natalie had summoned, along with the two ghost jocks who liked to heckle me. Coby drove the wraith into a marble gravestone, and the ghost jocks pounded it brutally.

Quarterback Coby quickly assessed the situation

and barked orders at the ghost jocks, and the three of them attacked the other two wraiths in a unified front. In some ways, they were better prepared than ghost-keepers, because the wraiths couldn't burn their skin— but they didn't have our abilities.

And wraiths were more powerful than any ghosts. While Coby and the jocks bought the others time, the final outcome remained inevitable.

What the hell's wrong with Emma? Coby asked Natalie.

But, of course, Natalie couldn't hear him. She kept yelling at me to fight, to help, and I kept standing there, watching from a great unfeeling distance.

The wraiths slammed through the ghost jocks, vanquishing them back into the Beyond. Then they leaped at Coby. He was quick. He faked right, moved left, hurdled one gravestone, and dove through another to land beside me.

What's happening? he asked. *Is it Neos? This place stinks of his power.*

I didn't answer. I couldn't get myself to form words over the melody in my head.

They're gonna kill Natalie, and then you. And then they'll—

A wraith slashed at him, and Coby twirled away and dove right at me. Right *into* me. He seemed to shimmer into true visibility for an instant, then pain burst through me, like a hundred wasps stinging me everywhere.

I screamed, and Coby's voice echoed in the agony of my mind: *Nobody can save them but you.*

The wraith caught Coby, slammed him into the ground, and started slashing at him with hooked fingers. But the pain and his words had snapped something inside of me. And for the first time that night, I knew what I needed.

My dagger.

I grabbed for the hilt in my pocket and leaped at the wraith pinning Coby. As I moved, I gathered all my rage and strength into a ball of lightning in my palm—then pushed the power into the blade.

A spectral edge of dispelling energy coursed from the hilt to the tip of the dagger, and I buried it in the back of the wraith's neck and twisted. A horrible death-cry tore through the graveyard, and the other two wraiths paused.

I didn't.

A ribbon of compelling power unfurled from my left hand into a noose that closed around the larger wraith and drew it toward me. It struggled and writhed, hands clawing at the path and the graves. It wasn't strong enough. I yanked close, like a fisherman reeling in a catch, and plunged my dagger into its heart. Its mouth opened in a wordless scream, and I snapped its neck with my elbow.

The final wraith screeched and sprang for Natalie— I spun the dagger in my hand and threw.

Sparks wheeled in the air as the blade cut through the falling light and plunged hilt-deep into the wraith's empty eye socket. The wraith melted to the ground, hollow screams echoing in the evening.

"Tell your master he's next," I said.

Then I pulled my dagger from its eye, broke its neck, and fainted.

I didn't remember the car ride home, except for one odd flash of conversation.

"I've never seen her like that," Natalie said.

"No one's ever seen anyone like that," Simon said, his voice hard.

I woke in my own bed in the middle of the night, and gasped in panic. Then I groped around in the dark, and found the dagger under the extra pillow on the bed.

My hand closed on the hilt and I fell back to sleep.

11

Nicholas woke me the next morning by stoking the embers in my little fireplace.

I watched him messing around until the fire started blazing, and let the events of last night filter through my mind. Our failed mission to find Neos's final resting spot. The arrival of the wraiths, as if they'd been waiting for us. How I'd frozen when my friends needed me most, and how I'd finally unfrozen into a frenzy of destruction.

I groaned and lay back in bed.

Are you all right, mum? Nicholas asked.

I burrowed deeper under the covers. *I'm fine. I just don't want to go to school—and stop calling me "mum."*

Didn't mean no offense, mum, he said, with a cheeky grin. *I don't think you'll be going to school today, though.*

My heart clenched in panic. Was someone hurt worse than I'd thought? Had the whole team not made it back? *Why? What happened?*

It snowed.

I glanced toward the window and saw little mounds of snow on the sills outside, and lines of sunlight glistening from the eaves. *Omigod. Are those . . . icicles?*

You never saw them before? Nicholas laughed in excitement. *I heard there's no snow in California. I can't imagine what that's like.*

He tugged a grubby mitten onto one hand, opened the window, and broke off an icicle. He crossed toward me, the icicle clutched in his fist like a sword. His sweet, childish face shone with pleasure as he lifted the jagged shard of ice. Then, in a flash, something changed in the air, and I felt threatened, like he was going to stab me. I grabbed my dagger and scissored my legs to pivot from the bed, slashing the blade toward him.

I saw the fear in his eyes, and stopped an inch from his chest.

He stopped, too, the icicle almost touching his lips. That's why he'd been lifting it—not to stab me, but to lick the ice like a Popsicle.

Oh, Nicholas. I'm so sorry. I—I'd never hurt you. I didn't— I'm still messed up from last night. I'm so sorry.

That's okay, he said in a small voice, and tossed the icicle into the fire, where it sizzled and melted.

It's not okay. I slipped the dagger back under my pillow. *It's not even close to okay. I don't know what's happening to me. I wouldn't hurt you, not ever.*

I know. You're not like the others. You care about us ghosts.

They care, too, I said.

Not like you. You're better than them.

But I remembered the feel of the dagger hilt in my palm; I remembered the jolt of pleasure when I'd snapped the wraith's neck. *I'm not as good you think.*

After Nicholas rose through the ceiling into the attic on some errand for Celeste, I pulled my laptop into bed, but didn't turn it on. I just sat there, lost in thought, until Natalie knocked on my door and shoved inside.

"Finally conscious again?" she said.

"Barely," I told her. "Are you okay?"

She sat beside me. "My neck hurts." She moved her hair, and I saw the welts. "Plus I've got a serious bruise on my butt."

"I'm sure Lukas would be happy to look at that for you," I said. "Is he okay? And Simon?"

She nodded. "Lukas bled a lot, but the wound in his neck was pretty superficial. Mostly we all got scrapes and bruises and a few burns. We got lucky."

"You were awesome," I said. "I can't believe you summoned Coby and the jocks."

"Yeah, who knew a summoner could actually *help*?" She lay back on the bed next to me and looked at the ceiling. "So what was up with you last night?"

"Which part?"

"The part where you stood there and watched a bunch of wraiths almost kill us."

I shook my head. "I—I don't know. I just froze."

"Like with the ghasts. Is this some Bennett thing?"

"No, I didn't even think about him. I don't know what it is. I just . . . zone out." I felt nauseated. "God, what if Coby hadn't been there? You could've died. I would've stood there and watched you die. You know, when I first started seeing ghosts, I thought maybe I had a brain tumor, or that I was going completely bonkers. It's like that, all over again. I can't figure out what's happening to me. It has to be the siren. I just don't know exactly what that is, or how to stop it from happening. It's not communicating with me the way other ghosts do. I don't know how to tune it out."

"Maybe Simon will know. Anyway, you redeemed yourself when you turned into Emma, Scourge of the Beyond." She rolled over to face me. "You killed all three of them in like two seconds. Where did *that* come from?"

I didn't want to think about the numbness and the violence, so I just said, "They pissed me off."

She giggled and, for some reason, that broke the tension. I asked what happened last night after I fainted, and she said Lukas carried me to the car and they came straight home—even though she'd wanted to take me to the hospital.

"Simon said you just needed sleep," she said. "He pretended he wasn't worried, but he's been locked in the study all night. I don't think he slept at all."

"Well, I guess we failed. We've got no idea where Neos is buried."

She nodded thoughtfully. "Have you noticed Simon's not that great a dispeller?"

"Yeah," I said. "I don't think that's why he's here."

Before she could answer, Lukas called from the hall. "Dudes, breakfast! I compelled Anatole to make pancakes instead of that tempeh crap."

I grinned at Natalie. "How many calories?"

"A bazillion."

"Sounds so good."

"Race you," she said.

I stretched in the shower, trying to shake out the aches and pains from yesterday. In an effort to look better than I felt, I ran styling stick through my hair, which really needed cutting, and glossed my lips. I put on a black wool sweater and my comfiest jeans, but my hair still wasn't behaving, so I accessorized with a black silk headband.

In the kitchen, Anatole was pulling a skillet from the oven, filled with something golden and puffy.

I thought Lukas compelled you to make pancakes, I said.

Oui, said Anatole, *but his mind is devoid of recipe. This iz ze Dutch pancake. Not your American flapjacks, which are ridiculouz.*

I told him not to compel you.

His eyebrows waggled. *Well, ze boy iz not so bad, demanding ze pancake instead of zat health-food horror.*

You wanted *him to compel you!*

He attempted an innocent look as he slid the puffed pancake onto a plate and sprinkled it with lemon juice and powdered sugar. Lukas and Natalie sat in the breakfast nook and watched Anatole slice the Dutch pancake into sections. I helped myself to tea, then settled beside them and dug in.

Lukas stuffed a second bite into his mouth and stared at me.

"What?" I said. "Is there sugar on my face?"

He shook his head, still watching me.

"Seriously, what?" I turned to Natalie. "Is it the headband?"

"It's not the headband," she said, daintily cutting into her pancake.

"Then what? Why is he staring?"

Lukas grinned at me. "I didn't know how badass you are. That's kind of hot."

"Shut up and eat your pancake," I said.

So, of course, he didn't shut up. Instead, he offered makeup advice. "You need like some crimson lipstick and black eyeliner. Oh, and you should get a tramp stamp."

Even Natalie had to snicker at that.

School was cancelled for the day, so when I finished eating I trudged back upstairs to loll around in bed some more. I was still tired from yesterday. When I opened the door to my room, I found Simon rifling through the wardrobe.

"Hey!" I said. "What are you doing?"

"Looking for drugs," he said.

"There's Advil in the bathroom."

"Right." He gave up on the wardrobe and opened the top drawer of the dresser.

"That's my underwear." I slammed the drawer shut. "I don't even smoke weed."

"What are you on then?"

"What am I on?" I was incredulous. "You mean all the drugs I'm doing when I'm not at school, or training with you, or practicing with the dagger, or doing homework, or killing wraiths?"

He crossed his arms. "Show me your hands."

"Why, are you thinking about becoming a manicurist?" I held out my hands for him to inspect. "Because you suck as a dispeller."

He ignored the insult and examined my hands, then exhaled deeply. "I'm sorry. I thought . . . the way you killed those wraiths yesterday, I was certain you were taking Asarum."

"What's that?"

"Wild ginger. An unremarkable herb, except for ghostkeepers."

"Oh, my aunt told me about it. Neos used it to increase his powers."

"It's like steroids for professional athletes, except more dangerous. And addictive."

"Why did you check my hands?"

"For Asarum stains. It changes the pigmentation."

"And you thought I was—" I was both mad and hurt. "How could you think I would do that?"

"What else was I supposed to believe after last night? First you stood there in a . . . a drugged stupor, then you cut through those wraiths like a—"

"A mad dog," I finished, and sat heavily on the edge of my bed.

That stopped him for a moment. He inspected me, and when he spoke again, his voice was gentler. "You saved our lives."

"I . . . I don't know what's wrong with me."

And I didn't only mean my power, standing there watching my friends lose a fight. But where were the people who were supposed to care for me? Somehow I always thought Bennett would be around to protect me. And where were my parents? Where was Max? They'd all left.

"If it's not Asarum," Simon said, "I think we need to consider the siren Max warned you about. Maybe she's not a myth."

I nodded. "I think I hear a voice, like someone humming a lullaby. But if a siren was hanging around, wouldn't I feel her?"

He ran a hand through his sandy hair. "I don't know. Hearing things isn't a good sign. We don't know what kind of power she has."

I licked my lips, because something else was worrying me, more than the mythical siren. "Simon, those wraiths last night. They were waiting for us—but there's no way Neos could've known we'd be there."

"Not unless someone told him," Simon agreed.

Not the answer I'd been hoping for. I'd wanted him to have some other rationale, because only the team and the house ghosts knew we'd be there. "Which means—"

"Which means you trust no one. Not even me. You're too important, Emma. You're the one he wants."

"I can't even trust *myself* if that siren's in my head."

"Emma," he said, staring at me, "I'm not sure how I'm going to keep you safe."

His words were so unexpected and his expression so heartfelt that I almost broke down. I crossed to the dresser and picked up the Barbie that had been lying there since I found her in my locker. I smoothed her shorn hair and straightened her skirt.

"I think that's my job," I said.

Later that morning, Lukas and Natalie dragged me downstairs, insisting that I needed to build a snowman, catch snowflakes on my tongue, and generally catch up on a snowless childhood. My peacoat had disappeared, which meant Celeste was trying to clean the wraith grime from it, so I grabbed a red down parka from the hall closet.

Then I realized it had probably belonged to Bennett's sister, Olivia. I flinched as I slipped into it, worried I might flash onto her memories, but I was learning to control that power—or maybe the coat was just a coat. And the gray knit cap I found in a basket on the closet shelf was just a hat, even though it smelled like Bennett.

I ran the cap under my nose and across my cheek, until Lukas said, "What are you doing to that hat?"

"What? Nothing!" I shoved it on my head. "It's just really soft."

"Uh-huh," Natalie said. Her tone made it obvious she knew what I'd been up to. "You're like a kitty with catnip."

I ignored her and stepped outside. "Oh my God."

Lukas and Natalie were at my side in an instant. "What's wrong?" she asked. Lukas stood in his compelling stance.

I gestured helplessly at the great white expanse before me. The drive was enveloped in a fluffy white blanket, and the bare limbs of the maples were highlighted with snow. Sunlight twinkled off the ice. "That's just the most beautiful thing I've ever seen. Like a Disney winter wonderland."

"Yeah, it's kind of cool," Lukas admitted.

Natalie scrunched up her nose. "Until it gets all brown and slushy."

"Don't ruin it," I said. "I just want to enjoy."

"Where should we go?" Natalie asked.

"Is there a pond?" Lukas asked. "We could ice skate."

Natalie gave him a look.

"Oh, right, bad idea." He stepped off the porch into the snow-covered drive.

"Wait," I said. "Have either of you seen Coby? Is he okay?"

"I think so," Natalie said. "He left after you fainted."

"I want to make sure he's all right," I said. "Should we sum—"

Whappp! Something hit me in the center of my stomach, and flakes of white snow clung to my coat.

Lukas laughed from halfway down the drive, as he reached to scoop more snow from the ground.

"Oh my God," I said. "Did you just throw a snowball at me?"

"You are in for it now!" Natalie grabbed a handful of snow between her mittens and dodged a snowball before hurling hers at Lukas.

I made my own and tossed it at Natalie. Game on. In the end, she and I teamed up against Lukas. He put up a valiant fight, but I'd grown up with a brother, and Natalie—well, she was just tough.

We called truce before walking into the village. The roads hadn't been cleared yet, and it was like the world had come to a standstill. We trudged through a foot of snow, marveling at the way it glistened in the trees and shrouded everything in silence, even the ghosts. The day felt like it was put on hold. I could forget about school, and no one expected me to be a ghostkeeper.

The café in the village was open, and I convinced them to get mocha red-eye chais. We sat in the warmth and watched the frozen white world and talked about everything and anything but ghosts. We were just three ordinary kids enjoying a snow day. I wished there were more days like this.

12

I wore Bennett's sister's coat again the next morning. The snow hadn't melted, but the wind had blown it from the trees, and the roads had all been plowed. As we trudged to school, I was less thrilled by the winter wonderland and more wondering how I was going to survive a whole New England winter.

Latin was miserable. Harry was completely hungover, and bragging about spending the snow day "Ad fundum*-ing" through endless shots of Stoli.

Coby would not be happy with him. Or with me.

So I sidled up during open conversation and said, "Harry, can we talk?"

He took a deep gulp from a thermos he'd claimed held chicken soup and said, "Abi sis, belua."**

---

* Bottoms up!

** Just go away, beast.

Vodka fumes rose from the thermos. "Don't you think you've had enough?"

"Quando podeces te regina eorum fecerunt?"*

Took me a moment to work that one out. And I was repulsed, once I had. "Harry, stop. We need to talk. Coby's worried—I mean, would be worried about you. You can't go on like this."

"Shall I say it in English, Emma? You are a human cancer. You are a scab and an abomination, and you ruined the best thing in my life."

There was no polite way to answer that, so I slunk back to my desk. Well, at least I'd talked to him.

Later that morning, I vowed to keep my distance from Sara in Fencing, but then I found her crying alone in the locker room.

Maybe I should've walked away, but I sat beside her instead. "Sara, what happened?"

She turned toward me, her face wet with tears. "Don't you dare be nice to me."

"I'm not being nice. I'm only asking what's wrong."

"What's wrong? Coby's dead, and Harry's drinking, and it's all your fault."

"So let me help you. It's what Coby would want. What are we going to do about Harry?" I asked.

---

* When did the buttholes make you their queen?

"There is no *we*, Emma. There's only *you*." Her hands balled into fists. "And he'd still be alive if not for you."

Natalie stepped beside me. "It's not her fault, Sara. She couldn't save Coby—none of us could. But we can help Harry, if you let us."

"Oh God!" Sara screamed. "Don't even pretend you care." She grabbed her bag and stormed out of the locker room.

"That went well," I said.

"Very," Natalie agreed.

After Sara left, we dressed in our whites and entered the gym. We ran through the warm-ups and watched Coach critique some other girls, then Kylee pummeled me for a while.

When we took a break, I sat at the bottom of the bleachers and looked at the ghost jocks. I hadn't seen them since the mausoleum, and I hated to admit it, but I needed to thank them. They'd done their best to protect us.

I guess it's time I learned your names, I said, *if you're going to fight wraiths with us, and all*. Okay, so that wasn't exactly a thank-you, but it was a start.

I'm Neil, said the darker-haired one. *And this is Lick*.

Neil and Lick? I said.

Our balls!!! they both yelled, and burst out laughing.

Grrrrr. I swished my foil in the air. *Forget it! I just wanted to thank you, that's all*.

Ah, sorry, man, the light-haired one said. *That's cool*.

Yeah, his friend said. *You're a bangin' ghostkeeper*.

Bangin'? I guess that meant they'd died in the eighties.

Whenever you and the hot chick need backup, the light-haired one said, nodding toward Natalie, *just call and we'll be there.*

Thanks! So maybe now we can be friends? I said hopefully. Because friends don't heckle friends from the bleachers.

That's not gonna happen, the dark-haired one said.

No, the other agreed.

Well, at least tell me your real names, I said.

Sure, the dark one said. *I'm Craven.*

Moorehead, said the other.

Ick. Never mind!

I'd never understand why boys were so gross.

The next few days weren't much better; then it was Thanksgiving.

My first Thanksgiving without my family.

Maybe that's why I finally acted on my plan to contact them. During Simon's lessons, he'd mentioned that ghost-keeping powers were changing. Or, at least, reemerging. Summoners weren't only able to make ghosts appear, but also disappear. Readers were learning to "write" their impressions and memories onto objects. Simon was beginning to think that dispellers could heal ghosts, too, and that compellers could free them.

So I'd been wondering what was possible for someone who could use *all* the ghostkeeping powers. I needed to find out. If Max was right about the siren, if he was right about finding Neos's grave and some "final rite" to unleash the full power of the amulet, I needed to hear what else he and my parents knew.

Thanksgiving morning, I locked my bedroom door and grabbed the red cashmere hoodie of my mother's. I could still smell her perfume in the knit, but faintly— more faintly every day. I sat on the bed and focused my "reading" attention on the sweater, trying to tap into her memories.

I found one at last, of her standing in the kitchen in the San Francisco apartment, wearing this sweater, while watching my father chop carrots for soup. I smiled at the sight of them, suddenly homesick and distracted from my plan—then I shook myself and concentrated.

I scrolled the image forward, like a movie advancing one frame at a time, as my mother crossed the kitchen toward him. She grabbed a bell pepper and he turned and touched her arm.

There. A handprint on the left sleeve. I placed my hand on that spot, and found a pinprick of my father's residual power. I focused on his power, magnifying it in my mind, then I opened myself to the Beyond.

When I summoned a ghost, I let the power flow in waves around me until I felt an actual presence. This time, instead of trying to draw something *from* the Beyond, I pushed something *into* it.

I sent a little pulse of power into the mist, a guided

Dad-seeking missile with a tiny message inside: *I need you. Please come.*

Then I pulled my power back into myself, having no idea if it would work. But I felt better for trying.

Downstairs, I found Anatole in the kitchen making apple pie while Celeste wiped down china that had probably been in storage. The day was gray, as usual, yet the kitchen was cozy and inviting, and the scent of a huge savory meal filled the air.

You made turkey? I beamed. *Real turkey, not tofurkey?*

Mais oui, said Anatole. *And ze dressing and my creamed onionz.*

I adore stuffing. Which was more than I could say about creamed onions. *Can I help you make the pie?*

Non! This iz not proper.

But I wheedled for ten minutes, until he grudgingly allowed me a crack at the crust. Under his tyrannical gaze, I gently rolled the dough flat and laid it in the enormous glass pie dish, then trimmed the sides. I felt like a kid again, molding Play-Doh.

I was crimping the edges when Natalie came in. "Oooh, pie! Let's make little leaves for the top, too."

Anatole eyed us warily. *Don't let her overwork ze dough. It will become flat and lifeless.*

I passed this info on to Natalie, and she burbled something French that made Anatole's mustache waggle.

What'd she say? I asked Celeste.

Celeste blushed—at least, as much as a ghost could blush. *Nothing that ze proper young lady need hear.*

We carefully rolled the scraps of dough and used sharp knives to cut leaves. After carving a few amoebas, we got the hang of it. We dumped the apples Anatole had prepared into the crust and laid the leaves on top.

Natalie clapped when we finished. "It's like Martha Stewart made it."

"Except her leaves would be botanically correct," I said.

Then we helped Celeste set the table. There were like eighteen pieces to each place setting: goblets and water glasses; aperitif, salad, and dinner plates; and soup bowls.

"Wait, why are there five settings?" I asked when we finished. "Me, Natalie, Lukas, Simon. Four."

Master Bennett, Celeste said.

My heart did a loop-the-loop. "Oh, is he coming?" I asked coolly, setting down some silverware.

"Is who coming?" Natalie asked. "And that's a soup spoon."

I looked at the spoon in my hand. "So?"

"So you just put one where the wineglass goes."

I ignored her and asked Celeste, *What makes you think he'll be here?*

She gave her Gallic shrug. *He's always home for Thanksgiving.*

"Have you heard from him?" I asked Natalie, carefully not dancing around the room.

"Who?"

"You know who!"

"Bennett?" She shook her head. "No, not in a while."

That didn't mean he wasn't coming. Setting the table was suddenly my favorite thing to do. The glasses, the silver, the plates. I loved every one of them. I loved the chairs, the tablecloth, the salt and pepper shakers. The napkins were perfect.

"You're humming," Natalie said.

"I am not!"

Her eyes twinkled with mischief, but before she could torment me further, Lukas and Simon burst into the dining room, their arms and coat pockets filled with large red and green apples.

Simon struck a pose and intoned, "'Even if I knew that tomorrow the world would go to pieces, I would still plant my apple tree.' Martin Luther. He had a point."

"Where did those come from?" Natalie asked.

Lukas grinned. "Thatcher."

"Simon, you stole apples from Thatcher?" I said. "What kind of role model are you?"

He gave a wicked grin. "An absentminded one."

"Well, you're too late for a pie," Natalie said. "We already made one."

"Hmm." Lukas glanced at Simon. "We hadn't thought what we'd do with them all."

Miss, Celeste said. *If I may suggest . . . a centerpiece?* She reached into the sideboard for a silver bowl with scalloped edges and a fluted stand.

"Voilà," I said, and helped them arrange the apples in the bowl. "Now *that's* Martha Stewart."

We sat down to dinner an hour later. I'd wanted to wait, because Bennett hadn't arrived yet, but Anatole claimed if we waited, the mashed potatoes *"will be like ze gluey paste."* So I was overruled.

I sat beside Lukas, with Simon and Natalie across from us, and the place at the head of the table vacant. I didn't mind if he was late. Just as long as he showed.

In an effort to duplicate my usual holiday, I insisted it was family tradition to go around the table and give thanks for something we were grateful for.

"I'll start," Natalie said, entering into the spirit. "I'm grateful to the Knell. I kind of hate them sometimes, but if they hadn't helped me, I'd be married to some old coot by now and pregnant with my second child."

"Whoa," Lukas said, looking shocked.

Natalie flushed and fiddled with her fork, oddly embarrassed by his surprise.

He looked desperate for a moment, then said, "Is it weird that I'm sort of jealous of an old coot?"

She laughed, and my respect for him increased. Nice save.

"My turn," Simon said. "Although you are ignorant children, you may have noticed I'm not American. Still, I'm willing to play. I suppose I will agree with Natalie."

Lukas scoffed. "Like you'd have a chance with an old coot. He'd never marry *you*."

Simon ignored him. "I'm grateful that at a time when the Knell suffered such a terrible blow, they still found use for me. And I'm grateful that it involves working with three such talented ghostkeepers."

"Aww," said Natalie, "who knew you were such a softy?"

"Okay." Lukas cleared his throat. "I'm grateful that instead of being sent to a home for disturbed kids for claiming to see ghosts, I'm living with people who are just as whacked as me."

Nobody said anything for a moment, and I knew Natalie was thinking the same thing I was. Lukas was one of us. His parents hadn't been there when he needed them most.

"Do your mom and dad know you're here?" Natalie asked.

"I told my dad I got a scholarship to boarding school. I think he figured if I disappeared, so would the problem."

"They didn't expect you home today?" I asked.

He shook his head. "Some pretty messed-up things were said when I left."

"Give them time, Lukas," Simon said. "My parents never understood, either, but we've managed to preserve our relationship. We just don't discuss it."

"Man, but it's everything though, you know?" Lukas said. "You try to maintain, but the ghosts are always there in the background."

We all nodded. We knew. Maybe that's why we all got

along so well. We all lived this double life, we all doubted ourselves, and we all knew how it felt when people in your family turned their backs.

"How about you, Emma?" Simon asked.

I thought for a moment, then sent for the house ghosts: *Could you come into the dining room, please? Yes, even you, Anatole.*

When they shimmered through the walls, I said, "What I'm most grateful for is you. My new family. The people who are actually there for me, day in and day out. The only ones who really understand me, and accept me, and . . ." I almost teared up. "If it weren't for you, I think I'd crawl into a black hole and never come out."

"We love you, too," Natalie said. She raised her crystal goblet—Simon had poured each of us half a glass of red wine—and said, "To Emma."

"To Emma," they echoed.

"And to all of you," I replied before sipping my wine. "Especially Simon, for letting us have wine."

I ignored Simon's look of hesitation. He was still worried someone here had betrayed us. But I knew he was wrong. This was my family. I trusted them with my life.

Now if only Bennett would walk through the door.

But he didn't. Not before dinner. Not during dinner. Not after dinner. He never showed.

I brushed my teeth and scowled at my reflection, then went into my bedroom. A moment later, I heard a tap on the door. Celeste came inside, her flowing red hair burnished by the light of the fireplace.

Maybe I should dye my hair, I said.

She pursed her lips disapprovingly. *Your hair iz lovely. And so iz what you say at dinner, about family.*

Thanks. I . . . you said he always came home for Thanksgiving.

If he cannot, he cannot. But Master Bennett, he iz a good man. You know thiz. Oh! I just remember. She took a small black box with a red bow from her apron. *Thiz came for you.*

I smiled happily. I loved gifts. Then I remembered Simon's warning about trusting no one—which came pretty naturally, actually. *Where'd it come from?*

The special-delivery man.

You think it's okay? It's not, like, some kind of spectral mail bomb?

I do not know theez words. I think iz okay.

I ran my finger around the edge of the black box and didn't feel any sense of ghostly resonance, so I opened the lid and found a nest of red tissue paper inside. Buried beneath the layers was an iPhone.

That iz not jewelry, Celeste said, clearly unimpressed.

I grinned as I grabbed the phone and turned it on. Weird. Who'd send me a phone? I swiped to unlock it and found a shoe-phone icon and I knew the answer. There was also a little *1* next to the mail application, which I touched with my finger.

A message had been sent to EmmaVaile at an account I

didn't recognize. It was from BennettStern at the same network.

Four words: "I'm grateful for you."

I felt my face light up with joy. *It's from Bennett.*

Iz still not jewelry, Celeste said, but she looked pleased for me. Then she faded away, leaving me alone with my gift, which I liked a thousand times better than any bracelet.

I tried to e-mail him back, but the account no longer existed. I flipped through the other applications and found the phone loaded with apps and ringtones. Then I clicked the music. He'd loaded a hundred songs, all of them about love. Some I recognized, some I didn't.

I plugged in the white buds and settled into one of the playlists. As the beats began to throb, I was grateful, too. Grateful he hadn't forgotten me.

13

On Saturday, we trained with Simon all morning. Then when Lukas and Natalie headed off for a run together, I worked with the Rake all afternoon. At least with him I could insist on hooking my new iPhone to the stereo, even though he hated every single song except for a couple by Outkast. Go figure.

I couldn't beat him with a dagger—not without using my powers—but I'd come pretty close a couple of times. When he finally sheathed his sword and vanished, my arms ached and my shirt was damp with sweat. But for the first time in weeks, I didn't feel completely spent after a spar. Maybe I was getting stronger.

I showered and threw on some clothes and knocked on the study door to talk to Simon, but he was buried in a book, as usual. Celeste was busy tidying, and Anatole was in a rage over seitan—some kind of meat substitute. I couldn't find Nicholas anywhere, to play video games or marbles.

So I dragged my laptop up to Bennett's room in the attic. I hadn't been up there in a while and it made me miss him all the more. Just the way the room looked was so him. Sort of casual, but classic, with its antique bed and dresser, childhood books and old video games. Though I wanted to snoop through his stuff, I knew he wouldn't like it, so instead I plopped onto his bed and stared up at the A-frame ceiling with its exposed beams.

I considered researching the amulet. Or Neos's final resting spot. Or trying to contact my parents again. Or checking into the mythology of the sirens. I still needed to figure out how I was going to tune her out.

Instead, I read a graphic novel I found in the bookcase. About twenty seconds after I finished and turned on my laptop, Natalie burst into the room.

"Do you even know *how* to knock?" I asked, embarrassed to be caught in Bennett's room.

"Why bother? It's not like you're ever doing anything interesting. Get dressed."

I eyed her. She was wearing black matchstick jeans, knee-high leather boots, and a magenta sweater that fell off one shoulder.

"Isn't your shoulder cold?"

"My shoulder is cold," she said, "but I am hot. C'mon, get dressed."

"Why, where are you going? Emphasis on the 'you.'"

"*We*," Lukas said, stepping inside, "are going to a party." He was dressed in his usual T-shirt and jeans. Not that he didn't make them look good.

"I dunno," I said, fiddling with my laptop, as Lukas eyed the room. He'd probably never been up here.

"C'mon," he said. "Get out of your black hole."

"It's comfy in here."

"Simon says"—Natalie gave the words a little spin— "we can't go without you."

"You mean he trusts *me*?" I said.

"Yeah. That's how un-fun you are."

I frowned. Considering me their chaperone *was* kind of insulting.

Natalie tossed a black miniskirt and tights at me. "Put this on."

"Fine," I said, shutting my laptop.

Lukas dutifully left the room, and I slipped out of pajama bottoms and into my tights and skirt. Natalie handed me a black long-sleeved T-shirt with red exposed seams.

"Not too much black?" I asked.

"Not for you," she said. I wasn't sure she meant because of my blond hair and fair skin or my personality. Better not to ask.

I took one last lingering look at Bennett's room, wishing he were here to go with us. Then I descended the stairs and shut out the light.

We took the Yaris. I drove, and Natalie gave directions across town to the strip of coast, almost like a causeway, that led to the Neck, the beyond-rich part of town.

"It's on the Neck?" I asked, worried we'd run into Harry and Sara, who both lived over there.

"No," she answered. "Turn here."

I took a right into a beach parking lot. There was a chain across the entrance, but someone had knocked over the wooden post it was attached to, leaving the chain on the ground. The Yaris rattled over the metal links.

"Are you sure this is right?" I asked, parking among a scattering of cars. "Whose party is it?"

"Anna from my Chemistry class," Natalie said. "She said they'd be over by the bluffs."

Outside, a chill sea breeze whipped at us, and I immediately regretted wearing my tights and peacoat instead of my jeans and down jacket. "Why didn't you tell me we were going to be outside?"

"Because you would've worn ratty jeans and that gray sweater. What's the point of a party if you're not going to look cute?"

I glared at Lukas in his jeans, big winter coat, and fleece hat.

"Sucks to be a girl," he said, smugly.

We plodded through the sand toward the bonfire blazing down the beach.

The thing about Harry's parties was that all the kids from Thatcher were invited. You never felt like you were crashing, even though his house was bigger than six average mansions combined. Everyone felt welcome, because *everyone* was there, even the kid who wore the green tracksuit over his uniform. To parties he wore red.

But a party on the beach was something more intimate. A dozen people sat around a fire built in the sand. Rocks and shells lined the pit they'd dug and filled with driftwood. Britta and her friends shared nips from a designer flask, and the guys cracked Rolling Rocks. A joint passed between two linebackers I recognized from watching football practice when Coby was on the team. I was sure they were big fans of mine.

The thing that really stopped me, though? Harry and Sara, sipping from a thermos they handed back and forth. I guess a flask wasn't big enough.

"Well, *this* was a bad idea," I said, backing away from the firelight before anyone noticed me.

Even Natalie paused. "Possibly not one of my best."

"Cowards," Lukas muttered.

"Maybe we should just go home," I said, hopefully.

"They're only human." Natalie bit her bottom lip, then turned to Lukas. "Dude, take one for the team. Suck up to Britta, so she doesn't pick on Emma."

"And what, you're gonna flirt with the linebackers?" he said.

She grinned. "If I absolutely must."

"They're not half as scary as Britta," he said.

Still, he obediently went in for the kill. There was something predatory about him as he prowled over and threw himself at Britta's feet. She made what was clearly a cutting remark, which he answered with what was clearly a joke. One of her friends giggled, and in another minute he had Britta leaning toward him, looking gorgeous in the light of the fire. I pitied him for the terrible sacrifice.

Meanwhile, Natalie spotted Anna and dragged me over to say hi. Anna was the type of girl who grew up to be a soccer mom. Cute and nice, yet very conscious of the social pecking order. She was pleased to see Natalie, not so much me.

I gave her a weak smile, aware of Harry and Sara staring at me across the bonfire. The smoke distorted their unfriendly expressions and gave them a sickly cast despite the warm glow of the fire.

I lowered my head, grabbed a beer from the cooler, and took a seat as far from them as possible, where the firelight faded into dark shadows. I nursed my beer as a dozen more kids arrived at the party, a few of them even sitting with me for a minute. Well, Kylee from Fencing did, and two boys who I'm pretty sure thought I looked desperate for a little attention.

I shivered and watched the ocean swells, checking out Harry and Sara every few minutes; they were getting progressively drunker. Then hammered. Then beyond wasted.

I wanted to leave, but Natalie's laugh sounded through the night a few times. She lived for parties, she loved dancing and laughing and flirting. She deserved a little uncomplicated fun. Lukas didn't deserve anything, because he was *still* flirting with Britta, but I figured I'd give them another hour before I made them leave.

Sitting with my second beer, I watched sparks from the

bonfire rise in a swirling column toward the dark sky, then fade away. I hugged myself, wishing Bennett were here to keep me warm. I wondered where he was, if he was missing me. If he felt as lonely as I did without him.

Then I heard Harry's forceful, cultured voice suddenly rise from the chatter. "No man is an island, entire of itself."

He took a deep swig and continued speaking, but I couldn't make out the words. I didn't have to. I knew the poem by John Donne—I'd read it in English Lit last year. Leave it to Thatcher to have a class drunk who spouts poetry. He turned toward the water and lifted his thermos high and raised his voice, shouting at the ocean until the other kids quieted.

Then he staggered toward the lapping water and despite his drunkenness his voice rang out in the cold evening air:

> *Any man's death diminishes me,*
> *Because I am involved in mankind.*
> *And therefore, never send to know*
> *For whom the bell tolls;*
> *It tolls for thee.*

He drained his thermos and tossed it into the waves. Then he started shoving through the frigid water after it, speaking again, though his words were lost in the surf.

He looked almost comical, walking fully dressed into the waves—but that water was freezing. I felt a deep stirring of unease. Something wasn't right. I looked back at the kids around the bonfire. Nobody seemed worried. Where were Natalie and Lukas?

I called to Sara: "Tell him to come back."

A girl I didn't know said, "Shut up, QBK."

"Don't be mean to Emma," Sara croaked in her deep voice. "She only wantsh to help."

Then she laughed hysterically. If possible, she was even more wasted than Harry.

"Sara," I said, trying to rub the tingle of impending disaster from my arms. "He's going to drown."

"Shtop whining." She threw an empty beer bottle at me, though she was so drunk she missed by twenty feet. "And start beering."

She found that hilarious, and the other kids around the bonfire laughed with her. I trotted into the darkness toward the water's edge, yelling for Harry, who was wading deeper and still reciting an inaudible monologue.

My shoes sank into the wet sand. I followed him along the shore as the tide dragged him further down the beach, calling for him and for help.

And I finally heard someone say my name: *Emma.*

"Natalie!" I said. "Harry's drunk, we need to—"

I'm here. I'll help you.

"Thank God! Go tell—"

And I realized I'd been hearing the voice *inside* my head. That it wasn't Natalie. The voice continued, *Don't worry. There's nothing to fear. You're fine, Emma—you're more than fine.*

For a moment, I thought it was my mother's voice—then Martha's. It was kind, with an undertone of strength, gentle and soothing as a lullaby.

"Where are you?" I peered down the beach, but couldn't see anything in the darkness under the dim sky.

I'm here. I'm here with you. Your family and friends, they're all gone, they left you, but I'm here. I'm always here for you.

The bitter wind stirred, and pretty lights shimmered beside me. The voice took on a girl's form. She was a few years older than me, with short dark hair, wide eyes, and scarlet lips. The girl from my dream. She smiled at me with even, white teeth, and I felt I knew her. She was like an older sister, who understood everything about me. She could take all my pain, my failures and responsibilities, and make them disappear.

That's right, Emma, she said. *You don't need anything except me.*

"We need to help Harry."

I'll take care of everything.

I smiled as my worries drifted away. For the first time in a long time, I felt at peace. I didn't know what I'd been worried about. She'd take care of me; she'd take care of everything.

From the corner of my eye, I saw Natalie approaching. "Emma?" she said, slightly breathless. "Are you okay?"

"I'm great."

"Do you feel that? There's a wraith nearby."

"That's no wraith." I smiled.

Save him! the ghost woman said. *Harry's in trouble.*

"We need to save Harry." I stared into the waves and didn't see him. "Oh God—where is he?"

He's drowning, Emma—he's sinking under the waves.

"Harry's fine," Natalie said. "He's back at the bonfire. It's you I'm worried about."

She's lying. She tempted Harry into the water. She won't let you save him; she's drowning him. It's her *fault Coby's dead. She's trying to kill Harry, too. Stop her, Emma—stop her!*

Omigod, she was right. Simon had warned me about a traitor—how could I have been so blind? It was Natalie. I'd thought she was my friend in California, but it was all just a setup to lure me to Echo Point. She betrayed me once. How could I not think she'd do it again? Was she still working with Bennett? Were they in this together?

"I was so stupid. I never should have trusted you. You set that trap with Neos," I snarled at her. "You're the one who called the wraiths to the mausoleum. I tried to stop you, but . . . what else have you done? Betrayed Martha and Coby? How could you?"

"Emma!" She reached for my arm.

I grabbed her wrist and flipped her onto her back in the sand. She gasped as the fall knocked the wind out of her, and tried to push me away.

Get her, I told the ghost woman.

She clamped her hand on Natalie's shoulder and dragged her into the oncoming waves. Natalie struggled as the cold water touched her. Her eyes widened as the ghost woman made herself visible to her.

"Hey!" Lukas yelled, sprinting closer. "Stop her."

With his fists balled, he summoned his compelling powers—and if he'd been a ghost, he would've been dead, because I would've shot him with the worst dispelling energy I had. Anything to stop him from hurting that ghost and ending her soothing voice.

Instead, I flung myself at him and knocked him to the ground.

"Emma! What the hell? What are you doing? She's killing Natalie."

"Natalie's the traitor. The ghost woman's saving us."

He twisted roughly and I caught a glimpse of the ocean. The ghost stood barefoot in the tide, wearing a short-sleeve black dress that came to her knees, impervious to the cold. She had Natalie by the shoulders and was forcing her head underwater. Natalie struggled, but was no match for the ghost's strength.

"Emma, snap out of it. She's drowning her!" Lukas shouted.

"Natalie betrayed us," I snarled, and punched him.

He drew more energy into himself, and I punched him again. Then he loosed a stream of power that caught the ghost behind her knees and flipped her into the water.

Natalie rose coughing from the waves, and Lukas, now lying on his side, compelled the ghost with a desperate barrage of force. When Lukas's blast hit, the ghost shimmered, and I pinned him to the ground, but he kept pouring his energy into the ghost until she faltered.

I get stronger every time they beat me, the ghost said into my mind. *Next time, I will save you. Once and for all.*

Then she escaped into the Beyond. And even as my mind returned to my own control, I felt her calling for me, so loving and intense that I regretted seeing her go.

Lukas shoved me off him, and I lay in the sand stunned by what had happened. What had I done?

Lukas helped Natalie from the water. He didn't bother waiting for me, but threw her over his shoulder and carried her toward the car. I trudged through the wet sand after them.

"Is she all right?" I asked, when I caught up with them at the car.

"Still breathing," he said. "No thanks to you."

14

Simon met us at the emergency room. They'd checked Natalie's heart and lungs and treated her for hypothermia. They wouldn't let us see her, but Simon had guardianship papers and they allowed him in.

He'd brought fresh clothes for all of us, and Lukas and I changed in the bathrooms. When I returned to the corridor, I found Simon pacing, looking overwhelmed.

"Is she okay?" My stomach tightened. "Tell me she's okay."

"She's fine—she's spending the night and we'll collect her in the morning."

"Can I see her? I want to tell her I'm sorry."

"She *knows*," Lukas said, stepping from the men's bathroom, drying his hair with a handful of paper towels. "You didn't stop saying it the whole drive here."

"I want one of you to tell me what happened," Simon said.

"She freaked," Lukas said.

"Natalie?" Simon asked.

"No, me," I said. "It was the siren. It was more than a hum this time. We could see her. And she spoke to me."

"That's a siren?" Lukas asked.

"She got into my head. She told me . . . she convinced me that Natalie . . ." I choked back a sob. "If Lukas hadn't stopped her, I don't know what would've happened. Face-to-face, the siren's too strong for me. I lose all control. She plays on my worst fears."

"That's why we're a team," Simon said. "What else happened?"

We went out to the car, and on the drive home we told him the rest. "Neos sent her to weaken me," I said. "And it's working."

"We'll stop him," Lukas said. "We'll stop them both."

"How?" I asked.

We both looked at Simon in the light of the dash, but he didn't answer.

Natalie returned home the next morning, plotting to become a candy striper in order to flirt with one of the doctors. In other words, she was fine. In fact, she was worried about *me*, so we spent the day lounging together with a tray of Anatole's goodies.

As we lay on her bed, downloading free games onto my iPhone, I apologized again.

"Would you stop already?" She quickly ran her finger over the surface of the phone, killing zombies on the screen.

"I just— Ooh, get that one!" I advised over her shoulder. "You know I don't want you to die, right?"

"You mean, in this game or in real life?" Natalie asked.

"Real life," I said. "You could die in the game, so I can have a turn."

The game switched screens to a new level and she grinned at me. "Too bad, sucker."

I smiled back, relieved she didn't blame me for the siren, happily helping her move to the next level.

That night, I slept the dreamless sleep of the glutton . . . until I woke with a start, frightened by the proximity of a ghost. I knew it wasn't Nicholas or Celeste, because they came and went without me noticing.

I pulled my dagger and Coby drifted forward. *It's me.*

Oh, thank God! I pressed my hand to my heart. *Are you okay? I haven't seen you since the wraiths. You look all right. Are you? I was gonna summon you, but—*

Settle down, he said, his ghostly face amused. *I'm fine.*

God, I just wanna hug you. Where've you been?

Licking my wounds. Those wraiths are nasty.

You saved us. I don't know what we would've done without you.

You would've lost, he said, with a hint of his old smile. *But that's me, Coby the Friendly Ghost. I searched the Beyond, finding out about Neos.*

Don't do that! That's what got Martha killed.

He gave me a look. *In case you hadn't noticed, I'm already dead.*

Well, but you could be deader. I don't want you any deader.

I'm not staying forever, you know. His voice was soft and gentle. *Once we get Neos, you're going to dispel me.*

I can't do that. Which was a lie. *I won't do that.*

Yes, you will. You owe me.

I swallowed and changed the subject. *What's the Beyond like? I've always wanted to know.*

Like a . . . a bad dream. Not a nightmare—one of those dreams where nothing makes sense. You ask for help, but your words come out wrong and the answers don't make sense. You forget who you are and what you're looking for. I can sense Neos, but I can never locate him—he hides himself somewhere.

We'll find him, I said, but my voice lacked conviction. I was still freaked out about the siren.

And what about Harry and Sara? he asked.

They're okay, I lied.

I've seen them. They're not okay.

So I bowed my head and told him everything.

You have to tell them the truth, he said.

That a ghost killed you? Sure, that'll work.

If that won't work, figure out what will. They're hurting, Emma, and they need you. His voice was cold and rough, lacking any trace of the sweet guy I used to trust more than anyone else.

I nodded, knowing I'd run out of excuses. And that I

needed to face up to the fact that Coby would never be the same.

He looked like he was about to say something more, but instead drifted to the window and *through* it, floating over the maple tree outside and twisting in the air before landing with his feet on the ground. I watched through the pane of glass as he vanished into the night.

The next few days passed uneventfully. A sad medley of school, training, and missing Bennett. Yeah, I had his play-lists, but they weren't enough.

Then Simon took a break from investigating Neos's final resting place to give us a lecture about the principles of the Beyond, but we were more interested in hearing how the search was going. Apparently William and Gabriel had come to the same conclusion as Max, and everyone in the Knell was trying to pinpoint the grave.

Well, everyone but us; we were training to stop Neos once they found his single weakness. If he had one.

"How hard can it be to find the grave?" Natalie asked. "Aren't there burial records?"

"They've all been expunged," Simon told her.

"So the body just disappeared?" Lukas shook his head. "They knew he committed suicide; they must've taken him to the morgue."

"I'm sure they did," Simon said, and his lips narrowed.

"What was that?" Lukas said.

"What was what?"

"That thing you did with your mouth." He looked at Natalie. "Did you see that?"

"Yeah," Natalie said. "There's something he doesn't want to tell us."

"I want to tell you what you need to know," Simon said. "If you want to defeat Neos, you need to understand the principles of the Beyond."

"I'll tell you what we need to know, Simon," I said. "If we're going to face Neos together, we need to know everything. Either we're a team, or we're not."

He didn't say anything for a minute, then nodded. "The Knell found where Neos had been buried—in California. They sent two teams. Two of the top teams."

"What happened?" I asked.

"The grave was empty," he said. "The body had been exhumed and moved."

But there was more. I could hear it in his voice. "And?"

"Neos was expecting them." Simon pinched the bridge of his nose. "They walked into an ambush. Wraiths, just like at the mausoleum—except they didn't have Emma."

"What happened?" Lukas asked, quieter than usual.

Simon shook his head. "We lost two teams."

He told us about the teams, the members he'd known, and though his face remained expressionless, it was clear he was grief stricken. He'd been holding himself together for us.

The Knell was falling apart. Yoshiro's death had staggered them, and losing two of the best teams felt like a killing blow. William and Gabriel were desperately trying to keep everyone together, trying to stem the tide of panic. They'd even suggested that our team move into the Knell building, but Simon refused.

"We need to continue training without distraction. I don't want to lose anyone in this team." Then he told us about the principles of the Beyond, which wasn't much more than Coby had told me. I tried to figure out how I could use any of it to fight off the siren. In the end, I decided to up my blocking skills. Martha had taught me how to shut down the voices in my head, but I worried the siren wasn't communicating with me in the same way, and that putting up walls would have no effect. Simon agreed to help me figure something out.

During the next week, our training gained a sense of urgency. We pushed ourselves harder than ever. Even the Rake noticed, after I slipped past his guard and slashed his arm. He told me I'd become a "tolerable" knife-fighter, which from him was high praise. Maybe I'd actually be okay.

We were dedicated, but it was impossible to maintain the pace, training three extra hours a day. Lukas finally snapped, and disappeared for an evening of Wii with some kids from school. Then Natalie insisted that she needed a shopping spree.

I finally broke down, too, but in a nerdy way. I stayed late after school one day, in an attempt to catch up on homework. I settled into the library, stuck in my earbuds, and cued one of Bennett's playlists, only engaging in a brief fantasy about what it would be like to study together. I bet he looked cute with a book.

At the other end of my table, some boys from my Trig class were discussing where they were headed for winter break. The Bahamas sounded good this time of year. Maybe the thing with Neos would all be over by then, and Bennett would be home for Christmas. I briefly obsessed about the perfect gift for him and came up with nothing. So I finally cracked my biology text and got to work.

At six, I walked back to the museum, only slightly freaked by the pitch-black sky. I was relieved to see the house lit up, and rushed into the warm foyer, ready to explain my absence, but it was eerily quiet. I'd expected Simon to come stomping in, demanding to know where I'd been. I hadn't told Natalie and Lukas about my study plan, because they would've joined me, and we'd have gossiped all afternoon and accomplished nothing.

In the kitchen I found Anatole stirring rice into soup, and asked him where everyone was.

Je ne sais pas, he said with a shrug. *That's why I make ze soup. So they may eat whenever zhey return.*

Weird. I checked my phone for messages, and found three from Natalie.

Hey, it's me, she said. *We're on the way to Maine. A ghost-keeper says he's been stripped of his powers. He doesn't know what happened. The Knell's sending us to investigate. Where are you? Call me.*

Her second message said, *Simon is so pissed at you. He says we'll be back by dinner. I'll bring you a moose.*

The third message, which she left twenty seconds after the second one: *Simon wanted me to tell you—* Indecipherable conversation in the background. *Oh, just tell her yourself.* Then Simon's voice came: *Don't go anywhere! Stay home. Stay out of trouble.* In the background I heard Natalie say, *Don't be so dramatic. You'll scare her.* And Lukas said, *You can't scare Emma. She does the scaring.* Then Natalie again. *Wait, did you hang up?* And the line went dead.

I looked at my phone. Another ghostkeeper had lost his powers? Just like Abby. The idea turned my stomach, because it meant there was another force in the world that we didn't understand. Possession, wraith-making, the siren, and now someone was stealing powers.

I started to call Natalie back when the front door burst open. I stepped into the foyer, saying, "I was just calling you. Do you remember my friend Abby?"

But it wasn't them. It was Sara, out of breath and frightened, her chestnut hair wildly disarranged. "You have to come right now," she said.

"Why? What happened?"

She clutched my arm. "It's Harry. He's on the roof at school."

"If bodysurfing in the freezing ocean didn't bother him—"

"He's not playing this time," she said, and her voice wavered with fear. "I tried to stop him. I didn't know where else to go. I don't even have my phone with me. You were the closest."

I pulled the red parka from the closet and slipped into a pair of snow boots. One good thing about becoming a ghostkeeper: I was learning to handle emergency situations. "Where is he, exactly?"

"The roof of the gym. We've been drinking up there between classes. I left him after school, but I started to worry he'd try to drive himself home, so I went back to check on him."

"And he's still there."

"He won't come down. He's talking crazy—worse than usual." She caught me with a desperate gaze. "I drove as fast as I could—I think he's going to jump, Emma. What if he's already—"

Her voice wavered on the edge of hysteria, and I found myself starting to panic. I couldn't take another death. Not Natalie, not Harry. Not any of them. But I still had a chance. One chance.

"He's not going to jump," I said, pulling the chain that held Emma's ring from around my neck. "I promise."

Tears streamed down her face. "The last time you promised . . ."

I'd promised her that I wouldn't hurt Coby. Instead, I got him killed. I swallowed back tears of my own. "This time's going to be different."

I shoved my finger into the gold band, and the second it crossed my knuckle, I turned into a ghost.

I didn't stay long enough to hear Sara's shriek of surprise. I flew out the front door and over the walls surrounding the museum grounds. Simon had explained that ghosts use some ethereal connection to the Beyond to travel. But even as a ghost, I couldn't venture into the Beyond. Instead, I thought about where I expected to find Harry, and then I was there.

Harry sat on the flat gravel roof, his legs dangling over the edge, wearing a long black wool overcoat. Just sitting there clasping an almost empty bottle of Stoli to his chest and smiling into the emptiness, the saddest smile I'd ever seen.

"I'm sorry," he said, to the breeze. "I can't do this without you, man. Not even for Sara."

He thought he was talking to himself, that he was alone—but he wasn't.

Coby sat quietly beside him. He glanced at me, then back to Harry. My appearance as a ghost didn't surprise him. While he'd been possessed by Neos, he'd seen me turn into a ghost.

The hardest thing is not being able to talk to them, he said.

Yeah.

But you can talk to him. Fix this, Emma.

I nodded and sat on the edge of the roof beside Harry, trying not to look at the ground, still covered in patchy white snow. We were a long way up.

I removed the ring. "Harry."

Harry started when he saw me. "How did *you* get here?"

"The question is, how did you?"

"I climbed," he said.

"You know what I mean, Harry."

He took another swig; then I eased the bottle from him and took his hand. It was like ice, from sitting in the thirty-five-degree weather. We sat there for a while in silence, the three of us watching twilight turn into dusk.

"Nobody understood why we were best friends," he said. "The All-American Boy and the . . . me. Whatever I am. But we knew each other, you know? We never had to explain." He wiped tears from his cheek with his sleeve. "How could I not know how unhappy he was?"

Tell him I wasn't unhappy, Coby said.

"He wasn't unhappy."

"Yeah. He killed himself because he was just so damned cheerful." He laughed, a hollow sound. "That's how I'm going to go, too."

"He wasn't sad, he wasn't depressed." I took a deep breath: now for the truth.

Tell him what happened, Coby nudged, before I could continue.

Gimme a second!

"He didn't kill himself," I finished. "He's still here."

"If you say he lives in our memories, I swear I'll take you with me when I jump."

"That's not what I'm going to say. I . . ." I shook my head. "You're not going to believe me, not unless I do something pretty ugly."

Do what? Coby asked, but I ignored him.

"When I was a kid," I started, "my parents sent me to an institution. A psych ward." And I told him the story, from when Neos attacked me as a child, to Coby's death at Redd's Pond. "And here's the thing, Harry. I summoned Coby back. He's a ghost, sitting right next to you."

There was a gasp behind us, and I turned to see Sara. From the look on her face, she'd heard most of what I'd said.

"What did you do?" she said. "You just disappeared. And now you're saying Coby's a ghost—"

"He's right here, Sara," Harry said sarcastically, waving his arm through the air beside him, where it went right through Coby. "You just have to *believe*."

"No, you don't," I said, removing my gloves and standing behind Coby.

You ready? I asked him.

For what? Are you going to hurt me?

Not you, I said, and pushed my hands into his chest.

Back at the mausoleum, when he'd dived through me to break the siren's spell, Coby had shimmered into visibility for a moment. Simon thought that because I summoned Coby—and because I'm *me*—we were linked. Just as Neos and I were linked through my blood, Coby was part of me, part of my energy.

And unlike any other ghost—the house ghosts or Edmund—when Coby's spectral form intersected with my real one, we established an interference pattern. Which made him visible.

For a few seconds, my fingers felt no worse than

freezing—then the pain started. It was like holding my palms on a hot stove. Waves of agony passed from my hands into my arms. I clenched my jaw and didn't move. I used just enough compelling energy to prevent Coby from slipping away to save me the pain.

"What the hell?" Sara said.

"Is that . . ." Harry dropped the bottle of vodka to the ground. "Is that . . . what *is* that?"

Coby began to glow, his skin and clothing taking a solid presence, his melancholy expression appearing to Harry and Sara.

Harry suddenly looked from my trembling hands directly into Coby's eyes. A look of wonder and joy crossed his face. He opened his mouth, then closed it again without saying anything.

"I can't," I said, between gritted teeth, "stand this much longer."

Sara stepped toward Coby, her arms open for an embrace, but Coby raised a hand to stop her.

Say something, I told Coby. *See if they can hear you.*

"Everything Emma says is true." His voice reverberated across the roof. "I love you both. Stop hurting yourselves. Live your lives the way I'd want you t—"

The pain overcame me, and I released my compulsion on him and jerked my hands away. Except unbinding myself from Coby wasn't so simple: a backlash of power blasted from the spot where we touched, knocked me on my butt, and made Coby fizzle into nothingness.

"Emma!" Sara bent next to me. "My God, your hands!"

I looked at my hands, then quickly away. They were a livid red, puffy and swollen, with blisters already forming.

Sara clasped me by the wrists and helped me to my feet. "We have to get you to the hospital."

"But Coby—did you see? Do you believe me?"

Harry patted the place where Coby had been. " 'There are more things in heaven and earth . . . ' "

"Harry!" Sara scolded. "Now's not the time for Shakespeare. Help me with Emma. Look at her hands."

He looked, then blinked. "Good Lord! That's one nasty case of phantasmagorical squirrel pox."

"Did you see him?" Sara said, suddenly smiling again. "Did you see him?"

"Figures he'd make such an offensively good-looking ghost," Harry said, in mock disgust. "But we have to take care of the living."

And to underscore the point, he burped vodka in my face.

Sara peeled out of the school parking lot in her BMW. I looked outside instead of at my throbbing hands as she sped along the narrow village streets to the hospital on the outskirts of town. My breath left steam on the inside of the car window.

"This is insane! How can Coby be a ghost?" Sara glanced in the backseat where Harry was sprawled. "Is he here now?"

"No," I said. "Can you turn off the heat? The hot air hurts the burns."

"Oh God, I'm sorry. What happened to your hands?"

"I get burned if I touch ghosts for too long."

She let out a puff of air. "I just, I can't . . . he's been watching us, hasn't he? I felt him. I thought I was fooling myself."

"He's been messing with my playlists," Harry slurred. "I keep finding his favorite songs cued."

"One day, I came home and found a whole stack of books on my bed," Sara said. "Stuff he gave me over the years."

I smiled. "He misses you guys."

Sara pulled into the hospital parking lot. "Where do I park?"

"Turn left," I said. "I was just here with Natalie when she almost drowned."

"That really happened?" Harry ran a hand over his face. "I thought she was being a drama queen. I'm such an ass."

"What do you mean, almost drowned?" Sara asked. "When did that happen?"

"At the beach party," I said. "A ghost tried to drown her."

"The one that killed Coby?"

"No, but that one sent this one. It's a long story."

"I can't believe we're talking about ghosts," Sara said.

"Because you are narrow-minded," Harry said. "I've spoken to you about that before."

"Oh shut up—you're drunk. If you were sober, you wouldn't believe a word." She stopped at the emergency-room entrance. "I can't park here."

"I'll be fine," I said, "if you can open the door for me."

Harry stumbled from the backseat to let me out. When I brushed past him, he fell to the ground.

"Oh God, Harry," Sara said. "We'll meet you inside, Emma."

Harry mumbled something cryptic about a bucket and a horse, then threw up in the bushes.

"Just get Harry home," I told Sara.

"We're not leaving you alone. Not after . . . every-thing."

"Yes, we are," Harry said, straightening. "Jeeves, take me to rehab!"

"What?" Sara asked. "Are you serious?"

"Cross my heart and hope to—" He peered around. "Is he still here?"

I shook my head. "Nope."

"In that case, I'm deadly serious. Serious as a heart attack. I need rehab, stat. They have a room with my name on the door." The manic light faded from his face. "And damn, if you don't take me now, I might start thinking I don't need to go."

Sara glanced at me.

"You know he needs to," I said.

Sara nodded and started to grab my hand, then remembered and touched my arm instead. "Emma . . . I'm sorry. We both are."

"I'm not!" Harry insisted. "I'm magnificent."

We ignored him, and I smiled at Sara, with tears in my eyes. Then they drove off and I stumbled into the emergency room. The double doors went *swish* and I caught the eye of a passing nurse.

I showed her my hands and said, "Ow."

15

The nurses wondered how I'd managed to give myself second-degree burns over both hands, and I told a disjointed story about confusing a pot of cold water with a pot of boiling water. They looked at me funny, but bandaged the burns and gave me a hard-core painkiller.

I told them I wanted to go home, then admitted I didn't have a ride. I couldn't work my iPhone with my fingers bandaged, and I didn't really want them calling Natalie in the middle of some ghostly event, so they left a message on the museum's answering machine.

They tucked me into a bed surrounded with curtain walls, even though I wasn't remotely tired. Then the painkiller hit and I fell asleep almost instantly, to the sound of crabby patients and crying babies. I dreamed that acidic ghast-drool was dissolving my hands.

Then a voice interrupted my dream. "Wake up, sweetie. We don't have much time."

"I don't want to go to school," I murmured.

"Emma! Wake up!"

I woke, groggy and disoriented. "Muh?" I sat up, and forgot the flare of pain in my hand when I saw my father and mother standing beside the bed. "Oh my God. You came. You're here!"

"Shh," my father hushed me. "They don't know."

"Who?" I asked. "Why are you hiding? Nobody thinks you killed anyone."

"Shh," he said again. "Let us look at you."

I looked back at them. There was more gray in my father's dark hair, and a stubbly beard marred his usually clean-shaven chin. He looked like he'd aged ten years since I'd last seen him two months ago.

My mother looked worse. She had dark shadows under her eyes, and her black sweater and pants engulfed her slight frame. Her face was gaunt and her skin jaundiced— she looked old and ill.

Fear clutched my stomach. "Are you sick?"

"I'm fine." She ran a hand over my hair. "You look so grown-up and beautiful. I like your hair." The short hair-cut she'd never approved of was finally growing out. "I've missed you."

"Why did you leave me like that?"

"To protect you from Neos—to draw his attention away from you."

"Well, *that* didn't work," I said. "How could you not tell me who I was? Who *you* were?"

"We knew you were special, Emma," my father said. "We knew your powers far outstripped our own, but we didn't know how to protect you."

"We needed to buy time when we realized Neos was returning," my mother continued. "We couldn't trust the Knell—we knew he'd corrupt them. We needed to keep you away from ghostkeeping until we figured out how to stop him."

"But you put me in a psych ward. How could you do that?"

For a moment, neither of them spoke. Then my father said, "We panicked. We didn't know—"

My mother laid a hand on my shoulder. "We were wrong. Does it help if we say that? We only wanted to keep you safe."

I took a deep breath, unsure whether I was ready to forgive them. At least they admitted they'd made a mistake.

"Do you know about our history with Neos?" Dad asked.

I nodded. "You were a team with him and Rachel." I blinked away sudden tears. "Daddy, when I met her, she was possessed by a wraith, and I—I—"

"We know," my mom said gently. "You didn't kill her; Neos did. Never forget that. In fact, you saved her, Emma, from doing even more damage to the Knell—and the Knell was her life."

I nodded and reached to put my bandaged hand onto

hers, and saw her fingers were tinged with purple, fuzzy streaks outlining her fingernails, like some strange bruise.

Simon's voice replayed in my head: *Asarum stains. It changes the pigmentation*.

"Oh my God," I said, falling back onto my pillow. "You're taking that drug."

"It's only an herb." She moved her hands away. "And I'm trying to save you."

"That's why you're hiding—because you know the Knell disapproves."

"The Knell's not in a position to disapprove," my father said.

"You don't understand," my mother told me. "We're trying to help you fight Neos. He's linked to me; he's using my powers. If I regain them, maybe he'll lose them. I've got nothing without this, Emma."

I turned to my father, a little dizzy from the pain-killers. "And you let her? Look at her—I thought she was sick, Dad!"

He swallowed. "I know—I told her not to, but she insisted and—"

"Get the amulet, Emma," she interrupted. "You need to take the amulet from Neos."

"Why? How?" I yawned, the drugs catching up with me. "I don't even know—"

"We don't know, either. Neos needs to perform some final rite with it—we don't know what, exactly. But if you take the amulet, maybe he won't get any more powerful."

"He's bad enough already," my father said. "We need to—"

"Someone's coming," my mother whispered.

"Wait! Why did you send me that note, telling me not to trust Bennett?"

"We knew Neos would try to infiltrate the Knell, and we thought he'd target Bennett," my dad said.

"But he's not—" I stopped midsentence. Was I sure that I was in love with Bennett? Yes. Sure that he loved me? Yes. Positive I could trust him? No. Maybe if he'd been here, but I had no idea where he was or what he was doing. Could he defend himself against Neos? Rachel hadn't been able to.

"Plus he's too old for you," Mom added. "You need someone your own age. Isn't there a boy at school, who—"

"*Mom!*" God, how could she annoy me already? We'd only been together like ten minutes.

They both stepped away from the bed. "We love you."

"Don't go! I need—" But with a *swish* of the curtain walls, they were gone.

The nurse checked on me as I lay there in a daze. My first thought when I saw my parents was that they'd finally come for me. I could forget all about ghostkeeping and go back to my old life in San Francisco.

But what was there to go back to?

I didn't want to be three thousand miles from Bennett, wherever he was. Or Natalie or Lukas and Simon. Or Harry and Sara. And would Coby be able to find his way through the Beyond that far? What about the house ghosts? I wasn't sure—even when this was all over—how a life with my parents fit into all that.

My friends needed me. They needed me more than I needed my parents. Which worried me. But there was strength in it, too.

"Oh my God!" Natalie shrieked, waking me from a dreamless sleep in my hospital bed. "Emma, what happened?"

"I thought I made it clear that you were to venture nowhere without us," Simon barked. He never sounded so stuck up as when he was worried about one of us.

I forced my eyelids open and found them surrounding the bed, worry etched into their features.

"Dude, killer war wounds." Lukas eyed my bandages. "Are you going to be all scarred and everything?"

I smiled, tears in my eyes. "I'm so glad to see you guys." I eyed the clock on the wall. 3:12 a.m. "What took you so long?"

"The ghosts were a bitch," Natalie said.

"What ghosts? Were you attacked? Have you been gone this whole time?"

"Yeah," Natalie said, "Maine is . . ."

"Freaky," Lukas finished. "The guy we went to see had, like, no powers."

I pushed my hair behind my ear with a bandaged hand. "Because someone stole them?"

Natalie shook her head. "Even before that, he was a total low-level. You would've scoffed."

"No, I wouldn't," I said. "I don't think less of people because they're not mega-ghostkeepers."

"Okay," she admitted, "*I* would've scoffed."

"*Anyway*," Lukas said. "It didn't matter. His house was totally infested with ghosts."

Simon explained that the man was in his sixties, and despite his limited communicating abilities, there was something magnetic about him. He'd collected dozens of ghosts over the decades—and they were distraught when he lost his ghostkeeping powers. He'd been living with them like roommates for such a long time, and suddenly he couldn't even see them anymore.

"The question is, who took the guy's powers?" Natalie said. "We could've used you, Em. Without a communicator, it was like a bad game of charades. The ghosts miming, us guessing—"

"Don't forget the old man wailing in the background." Lukas mimicked a terrible keening noise.

"What'd you find out?"

Natalie held up four fingers.

"Four words . . ."

She nodded. Then held a finger to her ear.

"Sounds like . . ."

"Oh, stop it," Simon said. "It was another ghostkeeper. As far as we could tell, some dark ghostkeeper snuck in, middle of the night, worked some serious magic I've never heard of, and when he woke in the morning his powers were gone."

"Neos?" I asked.

"That's what I thought," Simon said. "Except he wouldn't have left witnesses."

"Good point. And if he knew about Abby, he'd be using her against me."

I told them about how she lost her powers to some "cute guy." Then the nurse came with a wheelchair and rolled me to the door, even though I felt fine except for my bandaged hands.

We got into the Yaris, and I said, "Simon, how does that drug work? The herb you talked about, Asarum?"

"What's that?" Lukas asked.

Simon filled him in and then asked me, "You think Neos is using Asarum again? He can't—it's only for the living."

"No, but . . . what if someone else is? Would that explain the dark ghostkeeper? Like Neos, but without the grisly murders?"

A look crossed Simon's face, like it was possible.

"Who'd do that?" Lukas asked.

"Maybe Neos has a henchman," Natalie said. "Or it was that psycho siren who tried to drown me."

"Or my parents," I said.

"What?!"

I explained about my mom and dad. "But what if it isn't that? Maybe Neos just possessed a ghostkeeper to steal that Maine guy's powers. We still need the amulet, and we still need to know where Neos's body is."

Simon ran a hand through his hair. "We're no closer to finding his corpse. Maybe getting this amulet isn't a bad idea."

"Where is it?" Lukas asked.

"Embedded in Neos's tongue." I started fiddling with my bandages. "I'm not sure how I'm going to get that out."

"The dagger?" Lukas suggested.

"Ew," Natalie groaned. "Can I call in sick that day?"

"We need to find him first," I said.

Simon made a noise in his throat. "Or wait until he finds us."

16

Say what you will about Simon as a guardian, he got us to school the next day. I wasn't sure why he bothered, with the threat of Neos hanging over us—but I suspected that he felt that the illusion of normalcy strengthened us.

I answered a thousand questions about my bandaged fingers, which felt better already—achy but not awful. I looked forward to hearing Harry's outlandish explanation of the injury, but he didn't show for Latin. Which was good news. Meant he was probably at rehab.

I stumbled through the rest of the morning and barely greeted Edmund in Trig. He'd arrived looking peeved and severe. *Your friend is spending too long in the Beyond. Have you considered he might be leading you on?*

Coby? I said. *Leading me on? It's not like he asked me to wait for him to come home from the Beyond. We're just friends.*

He's delving into unwholesome things.

I still don't know what you mean.

But he refused to answer. Which indicated it had something to do with Neos. Edmund was terrified of him. Because Edmund wasn't an idiot.

Finally he said, *I'll tell you if you dispel me.*

Coby wants me to dispel him, too.

I asked you first!

I know, but I didn't create you. I'm the one who brought Coby back. He wouldn't be a ghost if it weren't for me. His spirit would be sitting pretty in his grave with the rest of his body.

Perhaps that would've been better, Edmund said somberly. *Neos has incredible power in the Beyond. It's not inconceivable that he'd influence Coby.*

I bore down so hard on my pencil that I broke the lead and hurt my damaged fingers. "Ow!" I said aloud.

Sakolsky turned from the board.

"The invalid's acting up," Britta said.

I shot her a look. Why did I have to suffer through two classes with her?

"Emma?" Mr. Sakolsky looked at me.

"I'm fine. I'm just . . . having trouble writing." I shrugged and showed him my broken pencil.

"Take a break," Sakolsky said. "I'm sure Britta will be happy to share her notes with you." It was always hard to tell with Sakolsky whether he was completely oblivious to social tension or benignly Machiavellian.

"Great, thanks," I muttered. Then Britta and I stuck our tongues out at each other. She always reduced me to middle-school behavior.

You're actually worried, aren't you? Edmund said.

That Britta's not going to share her notes with me? I think that's a given.

Don't change the subject, young lady. Sometimes he could be so schoolteacherish.

No. I trust Coby. I always have.

I hope you're right. Betrayal is a terrible thing.

He faded away then, apparently happy he'd planted the seed of doubt. I just wished I could keep it from budding.

In Fencing, Coach took one look at my hands and told me to take a seat. I climbed the bleachers to sit next to the ghost jocks, who were on their usual perch.

I nodded to them. *Craven. Moorehead.* Which sent them into peals of teenage boy laughter that almost brightened my day.

Actually, I learned a thing or two about fencing as I listened to them debate the matches. They were taken by a particularly flashy riposte executed by Sara against Kylee. As much as I liked Kylee, I wasn't unhappy to see her get trounced—I'd been on the receiving end of her foil too many times. And it was good to see a little pep back in Sara's moves.

Maybe I should try that. I fluttered my fingers. *When I'm well again.*

Nah, said Craven. *You fight dirty.*

Yeah, Moorehead agreed. *Can't teach that.*

You have to be born in a gutter to fight like Emma Vaile.

Raised by streetwalkers, the other said.

I sighed. Why did I even bother?

I moved across the gym and ignored them for the rest of class. Sara caught up with me in the locker room. She was looking better than she had in days. The accessories were subdued and her hair was in a ponytail, though at least it had been brushed. And she was even wearing lip gloss, a good sign when it came to Sara.

"Hey," she said with a smile.

"How's Harry?"

"On lockdown in Boston. I called his parents and they met us there."

"What's it like?" I asked, as we started toward the doors. "One of those glitzy rehabs with gourmet meals and maid service?"

"I guess, but it's still kind of grim. I just hope he's okay." Her rough voice lowered. "I think I need to talk to someone about all of this. I'm such an enabler."

When Harry was twelve, he went through a shoplifting phase. Coby drifted into view. *Sara drove the getaway bike.*

Hey! I said. *Girls' locker room!*

I'm dead, Emma.

You're still a guy.

I pushed through the doors into the stairs leading to the main hall. "Talking to someone's probably a good idea."

"Is that him?" she whispered.

"What? Who?"

"I saw you looking. I can—I can almost feel something. Is it Coby?"

Don't tell her I'm here, he said.

"Inside the girls' locker room? Does that *sound* like Coby?"

"No, he's too much of a gentleman."

I nodded. "Yeah, he'd never sneak a peek, or tell anyone your secrets, like that time you rode the getaway bike when Harry shoplifted."

"Coby!" she said, glaring in the wrong direction. "Promise me right now that you won't be hovering around the bathroom or I'll . . ." She looked at me. "What'll I do?"

"Ouija-board him."

"Yeah, upside the head." Her smile didn't quite cover her uneasiness. "Is he really here?"

Tell her I'll be good, he said. *And toss me that pencil.*

I told her, then I tossed a pencil in the air. Coby caught it—and it hovered there. He waggled it toward Sara, and she laughed, her uneasiness gone. Coby nudged one end of the pencil into Sara's hand, so she was holding half, and he was holding the other. They walked that way, holding hands through the pencil, upstairs and into the main hall.

"When can I see him again?" she asked, meaning like that brief moment on the roof.

"Oh, um . . ." I argued with Coby for a moment, back and forth, until he forced me to say, "Coby says, 'never.'"

She stopped walking, and gave the pencil a curt jerk. "What? Why?"

"'Because Emma can't do that again,'" I said. "I mean, that's what he says. I totally could, though."

The pencil started twirling in her hand, and Coby's

ghostly face watched her expression as she considered. She finally nodded, and waggled the pencil. "No," she said. "You're right, Coby." She started walking again. "Look at your hands, Emma. You did that for us—me and Harry. But once was enough." Her eyes outlined the space she expected Coby to fill. "What will he do now?"

"He says he's not going to linger much longer. He's got a few things to do—"

"No! He can't leave me. Not again."

Coby shook his head. *She has to forget about me.*

Why? She loves you. She wants you to remain part of her life.

Because I won't always be here, he said. *You know that.*

I told Sara, and to my surprise she laughed. "Forget him? I'll never forget him. Just . . ." She looked in his direction. "Just don't be in such a rush."

We continued that odd, three-way conversation until the bell rang. Then Sara rushed off and Coby vanished— and I realized I hadn't asked him about the Beyond. Or about Edmund's suspicions.

Before training that afternoon, Simon called us into the breakfast nook for a snack of pumpkin seeds and something called twig tea—which broke poor Anatole's heart. Even Celeste seemed a little downcast by the meager offerings. Only Nicholas, toying with the pumpkin seeds, seemed cheerful.

We ate and talked about everything. The Knell, the

amulet, the siren. The dark ghostkeeper, my parents, and Neos.

I dreaded facing him. Yes, I wanted this to be over, but sometimes I felt like the knight who has to slay the dragon to win the princess. Charging into a wall of fire with no weapon but a flimsy little sword. Just once, it might be nice to be the princess.

"So this is where we stand," Simon said. "We need to find Neos's final resting place . . . but we can't. Our second-best shot is taking that amulet from him—that, at least, will remove some of his power. And perhaps one of our readers can use the amulet to find his body. In any case, you're fully trained—or as near as you'll get. It's time to stop waiting, and to act."

"What're we going to do?" Lukas asked.

"We'll head to the Knell, tomorrow," Simon said. "Lay a trap for Neos, and wait till he springs it."

"What kind of trap?" Natalie asked.

"We'll summon him, if necessary," Simon said, avoiding the question. "That's why we're going to the Knell. That's where we're strongest."

"You mean that's where Emma's strongest," Natalie said. "This is all on her."

"It's where the Knell can best help her."

Natalie turned to me. "How are your hands?"

I glanced at them, still lightly wrapped in bandages. It had been less than twenty-four hours, but they were definitely getting better. It didn't make any sense, but maybe ghostbite healed faster than regular frostbite.

I bit the tape off my left hand and started unwrapping the bandages. "Just keep that siren away from me."

"That's Lukas's job," Simon said.

"What's mine?" Natalie asked.

"Summoning allies," Simon said. "And keeping Emma out of the wrong kind of trouble."

"How?"

"By keeping your eyes open. You and Emma have a bond. Sometimes being close to someone is as powerful as any ghostkeeping ability."

"What're you going to do?"

"Coordinate with the Knell. If we all combine our powers, we'll win this. As long as Emma is ready."

"I will be," I said, flexing my almost-healed fingers.

17

You look a mess, the Rake said.

After dinner, I'd slipped into the ballroom to summon him. *I thought you old-fashioned guys weren't supposed to comment on a lady's poor looks.*

You are hardly a lady, my little warrior.

I half laughed. Even the Rake didn't see me as a princess. *Well, your little warrior is ready to be a big warrior.*

He lunged at me with his rapier.

For once, I was ready. I deflected his thrust, and stepped in close. He backed and swiveled, trying to bring his sword to bear, but I slid under his guard and held my blade to his neck.

Passable, he said. *Again.*

My hand hurts. I switched the dagger to my left hand, shaking out my right, and he attacked me again.

Hey! I yelped.

Ignore the pain, Emma. Or better—use it.

I kept my distance from him, deflecting his thrusts and slashes and playing defense, while I thought about pain. The pain of my family disappearing and Bennett leaving me. The pain of Martha's and Coby's deaths. The pain of the ducking chair and of the ghostbite on my hands. Yet, here I was, still ticking like someone had filled me with Energizer batteries. Because the truth was, I was angry. That's what kept me going. And I focused that anger on the Rake until I pinned him three times in a row—and he finally declared me "adequate."

When we finished, we sat in the white linen easy chairs at one end of the room. The wall of windows was filled with black light, and I longed to shut the velvet curtains against the darkness, but was too tired to get up.

Yes? the Rake said, his blue eyes reminding me so much of Bennett's. The way he teased me reminded me of Bennett, too.

What? I asked.

There's something you want to ask me. I can see it in your face.

I'd been distracted by thoughts of Bennett, but, yeah, I did want to ask him something. *Was your Emma always brave?*

Not always. None of us are.

I—I'm scared. What if I can't protect them all? What if I can't win?

The Rake's smile warmed me. *Neos is right about one thing, Emma. You are the only real threat to him. He burns with raw power and hunger and hatred. But you . . . you burn brighter. You burn with life. He is stronger than you, but he doesn't understand—he* can't *understand—how fiercely you'll fight for those you love. You were well chosen, Emma Vaile.*

His sudden earnestness embarrassed me, so I said, *Even though I'm just a girl?*

Because *you are just a girl,* the Rake said, and faded into the ether.

The next morning, the light outside my window was dark gray: another beautiful day in Massachusetts. I rolled over for a few more moments of happily bedded bliss, and jumped when I saw Nicholas hovering over me.

Gah! What are you doing?

I sensed something, he said, his eyes big and frightened.

I reached for my dagger. *What? In the house?*

No. Yes. Outside—outside the gate. But not Neos—I don't think—not now, I mean, except maybe—

Nicholas! Take a deep . . . whatever. Calm down. Tell me what you sensed.

He rippled for a moment, then said, *Yes, mum. I was outside, and I felt someone powerful on the street. A strange man. I thought a man, at least. He stank of power, so I hid between the oak tree and the fence, and I watched. And he stared at the house—at your window, I think. For a long time.*

At my window, I said, my heart hammering.

Nicholas nodded. *And I watched and watched. Then he finally left and I—I stayed there, hidden. I didn't move. Not for hours. I was that afraid, mum.*

I tried to smile at him. *You do look a little . . . off.* He was always pale—I mean, he was a ghost—but there was a greenish tinge to his pallor this morning. *Then what?*

I crept closer to where he'd been standing, and I found this. He held out his hand to me, and in his palm was a small gray metal disk, like a flattened coin with slight indentations.

My spine tingled as I stared at the disk. I was getting some serious ghostly ping off it. *What is that?*

I dunno, mum. I thought a button at first, but it's not a button. I think he might've rubbed it, like a rosary.

The skin on my arms began to prickle and my ghost-bitten hands itched. I was afraid to touch the disk, terrified that I'd flash onto some awful place.

Nicholas thrust his hand closer. *Here, mum.*

Not yet, I said. *Go stand in the hall.*

Please, take it. I'm afraid of Neos. You have to find him. His eyes were wide and trusting, expecting me to handle everything.

I will, Nicholas. I just need to be ready.

I followed him from the bedroom and marched down the hall knocking on doors, and yelling for everyone to wake up.

Simon was the first to appear. He was wearing a white T-shirt and red flannel pajama bottoms. "Bloody hell, Emma, what's happened?"

"Does that really count as swearing in England?"

Natalie's voice came from behind me. She wore a black satin mini nightie, very sex kittenish. "I always wondered if it's like saying fu—"

"Natalie!" I interrupted. "Get dressed—how do you sleep in that? Where's Lukas?"

On cue, Lukas stumbled from his room wearing nothing but black boxer briefs. "Yo."

He caught sight of Natalie, and gaped—she might've teased him, except she was staring at him just as openly. Hoo boy.

"Hold up," Simon said. "What's going on?"

"Why's Nicholas showing us that coin?" Natalie asked, looking away from Lukas with some effort.

"Looks like he's begging," Lukas said. "Sometimes he takes this waif thing too far."

"He's not begging," I said, and told them what he'd told me. "There are waves of energy coming off it—can't you feel them?"

"We're not readers."

"Well, I was afraid to touch it without you. You ready?"

They looked solemn, standing there in their pj's, drawing their power closer to the surface. Natalie with her summoning energy crackling around her kittenish nightie, Lukas with his ripped bare chest—I mean his waves of compulsive force—and Simon with a look of grim determination behind his flashing eyeglasses, his dispelling power flickering around him.

I took a breath and swiped the disk from Nicholas's

palm. The ridges in the metal pressed into my still-tender skin, burning cold and hot at the same time. I felt a coil of dark power and then the whooshing, and the room began to spin, my vision whirling as though I were on a merry-go-round.

"Here we go," I muttered, and closed my eyes against the wave of nausea.

When I opened them, I was standing alone on a dark city street in a neighborhood of old brownstones. A row of bare-limbed trees lined the sidewalk, and a scattering of lights glowed yellow in windows, too dim to illuminate the street. It was quiet, like early morning. Maybe the same time as it was in Echo Point?

Was that possible? That this wasn't a flashback, that the disk was showing me someplace else in real time?

As I watched, the street filled with a thick silvery fog, and I shivered against the cold, even though I knew this was all in my head, and I was still standing in the museum hallway.

I looked toward a doorway with a cheerful wreath, then noticed a flash of movement up ahead. A dark figure darted through the mist. It looked like a man. He rounded the corner as I followed him across the road and onto another narrow street. The air smelled of dense moisture, and I tailed him onto a block of brick buildings with little shops and cafés.

I lost track of the man for a moment, then spotted him crossing a square and entering what looked like an old stone church with a tall spire. I stared at the sign in front of the building until it resolved into words: Cambridge Memorial Church.

I dropped the disk, and with a *whoosh* I was standing back in the museum, the disk rolling across the floor and clinking against the wall.

"Cambridge," I said. "He's in Cambridge, outside of Boston."

"Who?" Simon asked.

"I don't know. I couldn't see him fully in the vision. But this coin? It stinks of Neos."

"Cambridge," Simon said. "You think he's there now?"

I nodded. "Hard to tell, but—yeah."

"Then let's roll."

Behind his back, Lukas mouthed "let's roll?" and Natalie chuckled as she slipped into her room to get dressed. I told Nicholas to ask Anatole and Celeste to make coffee and toast; then I changed into black leggings, a long gray sweater, and my black boots. I beat Natalie to the bathroom, washed my face, and checked myself in the mirror. The girl staring back looked pale and tired and not at all ready to battle ghosts.

I cleaned my hands in warm sudsy water, then carefully rinsed and dried them before applying a thin layer of Neosporin. The right one still stung from sparring with the Rake last night. Like he'd said, it was only pain, but I found a couple Advil in the medicine cabinet and popped them anyway.

A knock sounded, and Natalie waited on the other side of the door, dressed in jeans and a leopard-print sweater, her dark glossy hair slung back in a ponytail.

"Really?" I said. "Leopard this early in the morning?"

"It makes me feel fierce," she said. "How are your hands?"

"Okay." I waved them at her.

She didn't flinch, so I guess they didn't look that bad.

"I'll see you downstairs. I asked Anatole to make coffee." I was strictly a tea girl myself, but Natalie loved her morning buzz.

I found Lukas in the kitchen, scarfing buttered toast, and I sighed. He no doubt had jumped into clothes he found on the floor, slapped on some deodorant, and called himself good. Meanwhile, I was trying to ignore my stringy hair, and Natalie was probably upstairs flossing.

Lukas swallowed when he saw me. "Dude, I got you something."

I grabbed toast and a cup of tea and eyed him skeptically. Why would he want to give me a gift?

"Here." He shoved a white plastic bag across the table. Another reason to be a guy: they didn't feel the urge to wrap gifts in polka-dot paper and pink bows.

"What is it?" I asked, half convinced it was a gag gift that would explode with green slime when I touched it. Considering the trouble he'd caused with the ghosts at his last school, I wasn't sure Lukas had grown out of that stage.

"It's for your dagger. I made it in art class."

I used one finger to pry open the bag, and nothing burst out at me. Inside was a dark brown leather belt with a tight loop sewn into one side.

Lukas shrugged. "I just thought . . . way cooler than whipping it out of your down jacket."

In the hallway, Simon bellowed. "Natalie! We're in a bit of a rush here!"

I slipped my dagger into the loop. Perfect.

Natalie stumbled in and grabbed the thermos of coffee that Anatole offered. She nodded her thanks and looked at my belt. "What's that?"

"Lukas made it," I said. "It's a dagger holster."

"Sheath," he said.

Natalie's eyes twinkled. "Are those little hearts stamped into the leather?"

"Gimme a break," Lukas said. "My teacher is pretty seventies. It was that or peace signs, which didn't seem apropos."

"Oooh, *apropos*," I said.

"Fancy vocabulary coming from a leather worker," Natalie teased. "Have you been studying for the SATs?"

Simon strode into the kitchen and glared at us, and we fell into an abashed silence. "I'm not going to have to put up with juvenile joshing this morning, am I?"

"Of course not," I said.

"You do realize we're after Neos?" he said.

Lukas cleared his throat. "Yes, sir."

Simon glanced toward Natalie. "No gossip about school?"

"Of course not. That wouldn't be apropos."

We all cracked up and Simon cursed under his breath. "Bloody teenagers."

18

"Watch out!" Lukas yelled in the front seat. "Other lane, other lane!"

I fell against Natalie as Simon took a sharp right, and I swear the wheels on the left side of the car caught some air.

When we didn't all die in a fiery crash, Lukas said, "Dude, where did you learn to drive?"

"London," Simon said calmly. "This is nothing."

"Right side, right side!"

I pulled out my iPhone and googled Cambridge Memorial Church, then checked MapQuest for the directions. I handed the phone to Lukas, so he could help Simon navigate from the front seat, then settled back. What were we doing? What made me think we'd actually find that guy I'd seen when I'd flashed on the disk?

I pressed my hand against the pocket of my jacket, feeling the shape of the coin through the fabric. The metal still echoed with Neos's twisted power, but I sensed deeper impressions than his. Maybe a faint tracing of Nicholas's touch—and mine, too.

There was much tire squealing and seat gripping as we entered Cambridge, and I suddenly called, "Wait! Stop! Pull over."

The car jerked toward the curb. Horns blared behind us, but Simon didn't seem to notice. He parked beside a No Parking sign and turned in his seat, looking at me expectantly.

I pointed toward the door with the cheerful wreath. "I saw that in my vision. I chased him past here. Everybody out."

Simon put on the hazard lights and we all piled out of the car. I stood a moment, unsure what to do. It looked like a regular morning in a nice part of town. No dark figures lurked, no tendrils of strange power coiled from the shadows.

We looked down the street, and a light fog began to move in, though the sun still shone. The fog seemed to rise from nowhere in particular, thick and silvery.

"Um," Natalie said. "That's not normal."

"No." Simon's forehead furrowed. "That's a spectral fog."

"What does that mean?" Lukas asked.

"That it's only visible to us, in the way that ghosts are visible, and will—"

"There!" I said, pointing, as the man from my vision slipped through the thickening mist.

I jogged after him, and Simon called, "Wait!"

When I glanced over my shoulder, the fog was already too thick to see them, ten feet behind. I said, "Over here."

"Where?" Natalie said. Then she blurted, "Hey! Lukas!"

"Sorry, dude," he apologized. "I thought you were a street sign."

"Yeah? Well, it says, 'No Groping.'"

Now *I* felt like saying "bloody teenagers." Instead, I called back, "Follow me—follow my voice."

I didn't hear them answer as I passed the block of brick buildings and little cafés and ran into the alley that opened onto the square. When I stopped at the other end, I heard a scream behind me.

"Natalie!"

I heard scuffling, then the thud of a body hitting the ground. I raced back through the alley, my power blazing, and tripped over Simon's limp form. I went sprawling across him and smacked into a trash can.

I stood in a crouch, my dagger in one hand and a blazing ball of dispelling lightning in the other, but there was nothing. No ghosts that I could sense, no waiting wraiths.

"Simon," I hissed. "Are you okay? Natalie?"

"Here," she said. "I'm good. He's okay—that thing came outta nowhere, smacked Simon into the wall, and knocked Lukas on his butt."

Simon groaned. "Did you feel his power?"

"I felt his right hook," Lukas said, cupping his bloody nose in his hand.

"I don't know what that was," Simon said, "but it was powerful."

"Stay here," I told Natalie. "Keep them safe."

"Me? I'm a summoner—what can I do?"

"I don't know," I said, trotting away. "But you're the only one still standing."

Across from the alley, I found the Cambridge Memorial Church, just like in my vision—and now I felt a hard swirl of power inside.

I didn't stop running until I reached the front doors. They were grand and imposing, made of ancient oak with iron latches. I paused and caught my breath and drew my energy close.

Maybe I should've waited for the team, but my spine tingled with warning as ghostly energy radiated down my arms to my fingertips. Something very powerful was inside the church.

I opened the door and the fog billowed around me through the doorway, then dissipated in the church. Stained-glass windows lined the walls, and rows of pale wooden pews led to an intricately designed dais.

I slunk to one side of the room and crept forward, the rubber soles on my boots completely silent. I passed a little niche with candles and considered lighting one for strength. I had no idea what I was facing. By the time I reached the podium in front, my hand throbbed from gripping my dagger, and my breath sounded harsh in the enormous empty room.

Three steps later, a dark shape launched at me from behind a curtain.

I slashed with my dagger as his fist came flying at my

face before stopping an inch away. I didn't wonder at his hesitation, because I was already pivoting and sweeping his feet from beneath him.

He slammed to the ground and said, "Emma!"

I looked down and was shocked at my discovery. "Oh my God. Bennett! What are you doing here?"

"Getting my butt kicked." He stood with a grunt. "How about you?"

"Chasing some new kind of wraith or something. There's this spectral fog . . . we don't know what's behind it."

"I know. I got lost in it outside. Something was following me. I couldn't see what I was doing, couldn't dispel, so I knocked them down and took refuge here."

"Wait," I said. "That was you? That was us, Bennett. Didn't you recognize Natalie?"

His face darkened. "Was that her?"

I frowned. "How could you not—"

"This isn't really how I imagined our reunion." He half smiled.

"Yeah." I couldn't believe he was here. That *he* had been the figure in my vision. He'd seemed so villainous. I'd thought he must be Neos.

"Is that my sister's jacket?" he asked.

"Oh. Yeah, sorry. Natalie said I should get a new one, but—"

"That's okay," he said, his gaze intent on my face, like he was trying to memorize me. "She'd want you to have it."

He looked like he'd lost weight, his cheekbones more

defined and dark circles under his eyes. Still, those cobalt blue eyes—I could lose myself in them forever. Okay, so maybe I didn't completely trust him; that didn't mean I didn't still need him. I stepped closer, wanting to throw my arms around him, bury my face in his neck, and smell his boy scent that was so familiar and foreign at the same time.

I managed to restrain myself, and he brushed my hair back with his hand. I felt my heart hammering again—but no longer from fear.

"That looks dangerous." He nodded toward my dagger.

I sheathed it. "It was Emma's."

"Oh, right." He nodded. "From the battle of the ghasts."

"Who reports to you?" I asked. "The Knell, or Natalie?"

"Are they telling me anything you don't want me to know?" His tone was teasing and unrepentant about spying on me.

"No." But I wasn't telling the whole truth. I couldn't get over my parents' distrust of him. The little seed of doubt they'd planted.

I started to say more, when the front door of the church opened. "That must be Natalie and the others," I said.

"Come here." He took my hand and led me behind the curtain. "I'm not done with you yet."

I liked the sound of that. We climbed stairs that led to a galley overlooking the room below, and Bennett drew me into a secluded nook, hidden from anyone entering the building.

I licked my lips as he pulled me closer, tracing my hair with his fingers. "I missed you," he said. "Every day. Every night."

"Me, too." I moved to kiss him, but up close he looked even more exhausted, his skin and his eyes ringed with red. I stopped. "Are you all right?"

"I am now that you're here."

"You look terrible, Bennett, you look—"

He kissed me and I forgot everything but the touch of his lips and the feel of his hands. I stroked him with my eyes half closed . . . then noticed his fingers.

His nails had turned purple. A chill spread in my chest. "What are you doing?"

He saw me staring at his hands, and pulled them away. "It makes me stronger, Emma. It's the only way to stop Neos. To be with you."

"Simon says Asarum is addictive. And deadly."

"Not as deadly as facing Neos without my full powers. I'm stronger than ever." He loosed a glow of power. "I can help you bring him down."

I swallowed. "It's you, isn't it? You're the one stealing powers from ghostkeepers. You went to Abby and . . . and that guy in Maine, and—"

"I won't let you face Neos alone," he said.

"You're gonna kill yourself with this stuff. Look at you."

"I'd die for you."

I could see the truth in his eyes. "No, Bennett. I don't *want* you to die for me! I want us to live for each other, I want—"

Natalie's voice called out from below. "Emma? Emma, where are you?"

"We're here!" I cried.

"Don't go," Bennett begged, taking my arm.

I couldn't help staring at his hands. "I have to. They're worried."

"Don't be angry. There was no other way."

"I'm not angry. I just . . . you look like you're dying and—will you stop? You're strong enough."

"Not yet," he said. "Not until he's gone."

I shook my head, tears in my eyes, as Natalie and the others called my name below. "I can't do this without you," I said. "I need you, I need you with me."

His eyes held something suddenly fierce. "They expect you to do everything. Let Emma fight, let Emma die. I'm not just here to hold your hand, Emma, I'm here to fight beside you. And if this is what it takes—"

"Where are you?" Natalie called.

"I'm here," I yelled, still looking at Bennett and blinking back tears. "Upstairs."

"I love you," he said. "Never doubt that."

I pressed my lips against his, trying to compress all my love and worries and desires into one little kiss. We lingered a moment, cheeks pressed together, skin to skin, my hand pressed against his beating heart, neither of us wanting to let go.

"Emma!" Simon yelled. "Report in now!"

I buried my face in his neck one last time, then stepped from the nook and leaned against the railing of the galley, where I saw the team spread out among the pews in the room. Simon's training was evident in how they kept their backs to each other, prepared for any attack.

"Up here," I said. "I'm okay. I'm coming down."

I heard the galley door close behind me and didn't even turn around. I knew he was gone.

19

We sat on the cold stone stairs in front of the church and I told them everything—almost.

I'd never been one of those girls who obsessed about guys, who made drama over every imagined slight and inconsiderate remark. Or the kind of girl who totally changed herself to make a boy happy. And I certainly didn't fall apart without a boyfriend, turning into some empty shell.

But at that moment, I would've done anything to see Bennett again. To hold him and heal him. To turn back time and keep him from resorting to Asarum—he'd only taken it to help me. I would've done anything to lose the curse of my powers and live a normal life. With him.

I told them everything except how much I was willing to sacrifice to be with Bennett.

"So your boyfriend is a junkie?" Lukas asked.

Natalie elbowed him. "Not helping."

"What'll happen to him?" I asked Simon.

"I've heard cases of ghostkeepers kicking the habit—if they stop soon enough. Before they . . ." He trailed off.

"Before they what?"

"Gain too much power. Which Bennett already has. He's turning himself into something terrible, Emma. We thought he was *Neos*."

"But he wasn't," Natalie said. "Let's think about this a minute." She tapped a fingernail against the steps a few times, then asked me, "What did Bennett say about that disk that led us here?"

I shook my head. "I didn't ask."

"So are we sure that was him, standing outside the fence, watching your room?"

"Nicholas would've recognized him," I said.

"And Emma said she felt Neos on the disk," Lukas posed. "And where'd the fog come from?"

We sat in a stupefied silence for a minute, then Simon said, "The timing is odd. Finding that disk the morning we planned to head to the Knell."

"And the fact that Bennett—or whoever—just dropped it there is pretty convenient," Natalie said. "What if . . . what if it was a distraction?"

"To get us away from the museum," Simon mused.

"What would Neos want with the museum?" Lukas asked.

"The Knell thinks he needs some final rite. Could it have something to do with that?" I wondered.

"Or maybe he's after my books?" Simon said.

"Yeah, that's Neos's big secret." Lukas lowered his voice. "He doesn't have a library card."

"Some of those books are extremely rare," Simon said stiffly.

"What else is at the museum that he can use against Emma?" Natalie asked.

"Hostages," I said, suddenly realizing. "Nicholas and Celeste and Anatole."

We all stood abruptly and ran toward the car. This time, none of us complained about Simon's driving.

We spent an hour stuck in traffic, even though I urged Simon to drive in the breakdown lane. Then I barely waited for the wheels to stop in the gravel drive before sprinting into the museum. I stood in the foyer calling for each of them. When nobody answered, I closed my eyes and summoned them. Celeste shimmered into existence first, quickly followed by Anatole, both of them looking terrified.

Natalie entered behind me. "Where's Nicholas?" she asked.

Celeste's eyes were wide, having understood Natalie. *He's gone.*

Where? I asked. *How?*

We do not know. We felt a . . . a rip in the Beyond.

He took him, Anatole said. *He took him from ze house. I*

thought we were bound to stay inside ze gate, but he took him. He reached and poof. No more Nicholas.

Celeste wrung her hands. *Ze poor boy.*

Who took him? Neos?

Oui, Celeste said. *Nobody else haz this much power.*

There was nothing we could do, Anatole added. *We didn't want him to take us, too—to use us against you. We fled.*

I'm glad you did, I said, then turned to the others. "Neos grabbed him. He's gone."

"How long ago?" Simon asked. "Can you summon him?"

"I don't know." I asked the ghosts if they thought there was time to find Nicholas before Neos took him too far into the Beyond.

Perhapz, if you press on the mushroom, Celeste said.

What?

It iz expression français, Anatole said. *She means hurry.*

Natalie and I decided to hold hands, to see if we could combine our strength, but it was clear we approached summoning completely differently. When I pushed, she pulled, and when I listened, she spoke. We looked at each other oddly, then I dropped her hand and said, "I'll be over there," before moving to the other side of the room.

"Yeah," she said, then got back to work.

I closed my eyes and tuned my energy toward summoning. It didn't feel like lightning, the way compelling and dispelling did, more like listening to the hum of the world, focusing on a familiar voice in a crowd.

I threw myself further into the power than ever, but

didn't hear a whisper of Nicholas. I did feel a comfortable presence, though, and Coby materialized beside me.

Hey, Coby said, *give a ghost a break. I was just haunting a DVD in Sara's history class.*

You can do that? Celeste said. *Haunt ze television?*

We cannot, Anatole said sadly, like all he ever wanted was to appear in an episode of *Law & Order*.

Well, I'm an Emma Vaile production, Coby explained. *What you do is, you focus on the—*

Coby! I interrupted. *Neos kidnapped Nicholas.*

The little waif guy?

Yeah—can you help us find him?

Gimme a second. He vanished, and I explained to Simon and the others that he was searching. He reappeared a moment later.

Nicholas isn't in the Beyond, he said. *And I can't even feel Neos. I can* always *feel Neos, because he's so powerful, but suddenly he's just . . . gone.*

"Okay," I said. "Nicholas isn't in the Beyond, and he's not here. Neos must be holding him somewhere."

"He'll contact us soon," Simon said. "There's no reason to kidnap Nicholas unless he issues demands."

"He's going to want Emma," Natalie said. "And she'll agree to meet him alone."

"We'll lock you in the basement before we let that happen," Lukas told me.

Clearly this was something they'd discussed. "That's not what concerns me," Simon said. "I'm worried about the timing. The morning we're going to head to the Knell, we're blindsided by all of this. Neos knew our plans when we did."

"How?" Natalie asked.

Simon didn't mention his fear of a traitor. He just said, "If he knew we were going to the Knell, this is all a distraction."

"To keep us away from the museum while he snatched Nicholas," Natalie said. "Or to keep us away from the Knell?"

"Perhaps both," Simon said.

Then it hit me. "I know where Neos is. I know why he kept us away from the Knell. That's the only place he can hide completely. They told me the building is shielded— so protected that even ghostkeepers can't tell what's going on inside."

"He's there already?" Lukas asked.

"Yeah, that's why he sent us to Cambridge—and lost us in that fog, hoping we'd fight Bennett. He must've planted the coin that Nicholas found—that's why I felt him. He knew we were heading to the Knell, and he needed to get there first."

"To do what?" Natalie asked.

"Nothing pleasant," Simon said. "Let's go."

I noticed Natalie biting her lip, suddenly looking young and unsure. "Maybe you should stay here, in case Nicholas makes it back," I told her.

"No," she answered in a small voice. "I'm staying with you."

"Lukas?" I asked.

"My policy is, stick with the hot chicks." Then he fiddled with the stair railing and added, "And you guys are my family now—I'm not letting you down."

"If I could," Simon said, "I'd make you all stay. But we're a team. None of us can do this alone, not even Emma."

I glanced at Coby. *Can you get to New York?*

He nodded. *This is it, huh? After this it'll all be over.*

I hope so. And then I'll . . . do what you want. Even if that meant dispelling him.

I know you will, Emma, he said, relief in his eyes.

"We are so going to blow Neos's mind," Natalie said, her cockiness back, "when we show up in the electric blue tin can. Now *that* is a threat."

"I was thinking about that," Simon said, and pushed into Mr. Stern's office. He reappeared a moment later dangling keys from one finger. "I found these. A Porsche, I believe."

"How are we all going to fit in a Porsche?" Lukas asked.

"It's a Cayenne," Simon said. "The SUV."

Natalie grinned. "Now, that's more like it."

We were ready for battle. We were eager, we were angry, we were trained.

Then we were bored. Three hours in the car kind of takes the edge off.

Simon insisted on listening to the Bach CD that was already in the Porsche's player, so Natalie and Lukas immediately wired up and stared out the windows, listening to their own music. Me, I kind of liked classical music, which reminded me of my dad, but I liked Bennett's playlist more.

I cued up a song, then texted my mom and Max, though I wasn't even sure my mom knew how to get her texts. I didn't expect my family to help, but I wanted them to know what I was facing. And I wanted them to know that I cared. Even though they completely sucked as a family.

Then I texted Bennett. I didn't know what to say. He already knew everything that mattered—but I guess I wasn't trying to tell him something he didn't know, just something true. After half a dozen false starts, I wrote: I love you. Which felt trite, but nothing else mattered.

My hands ached when I finished, the skin still tender from ghostburns. I put the window down and cooled them in the breeze until Natalie yelled at me to shut the window; then we ate trail mix and apples in silence.

I couldn't bear for a single one of them to get hurt. And I knew they'd do as much as they could, but I kept thinking of that tapestry hanging at the Knell. It all came down to me. This was my fight. Was I strong and brave enough to defeat him?

In the front seat, Lukas said, "Get off here."

We spent twenty minutes lost in the city, then finally found the right neighborhood. I recognized the narrow streets and quaint shops.

"Have you guys been here before?" I asked.

"Only once," Natalie said. "I never knew there was a real headquarters until Bennett finally brought me."

"Once for me, too," Lukas said. "This street is seriously old."

Simon smiled. "You ought to visit Europe. Our ghosts go way back."

"I've never been to Europe." Natalie's voice was wistful, probably wondering if she'd ever have the chance.

"I always wanted to go to Amsterdam," Lukas said.

Natalie and I shared a look. Every teenage boy's fantasy. Legal weed and the red-light district.

"To see the Van Gogh museum, right?" Simon said, only he pronounced it "Van Goff."

"Uh . . ."

"He means Van Gogh," I said.

"Oh, right," Lukas said. "Yeah, I want to see the paintings."

We all smiled knowingly. Then we were there. We rounded the corner and the Knell fortress glared at us from the end of the block.

Lukas stared at the shuttered houses and empty park. "Dude, last time I was here—"

"There were ghosts," I finished. "Ghosts everywhere. And ghostkeepers."

"What happened to them?" Natalie asked.

"They're hiding from Neos," I said. "He's here."

Simon parked in front of the Knell and turned off the

engine. None of us opened a door. We just sat there quietly, looking at the house.

Natalie finally broke the silence. "I really like this car."

It was enough to spur me into action. "Okay," I said. "Let's go slay a ghost."

20

We crept past the ornate iron gates into the shadow of the looming trees, then stopped short. One step onto the grounds, and the impact of Neos's cruel power hit us like a rock, his darkness seeping through every brick and blade of grass.

Lukas swore, and I nodded in agreement. Neos was strong—much stronger than when I'd faced him the last time.

Simon said, "Remember your training. Our job is to get Emma close enough to Neos to end him."

"Oh, is that all?" Lukas said.

"Lukas, you take the siren when she attacks Emma. Natalie, you summon our allies—and keep an eye on Emma; you know her best. We've got to keep her from getting drawn into other fights. I'll dispel any immediate threat."

I drew my dagger as we approached the front doors. No ghostly servants this time, no sign of any activity.

And the doors were open wide in invitation. Neos was waiting for us.

We looked at each other, but nobody said anything. We just stepped inside and wandered the marble halls filled with antiquities. The house was stifling hot, and we shed our coats and tossed them on a wooden settee.

There was no way Neos didn't know we were here, and I couldn't help wishing we were better prepared. That we'd laid a trap for him. Instead, we were scrambling around like idiots in a horror film.

Waiting to be picked off one by one.

We stalked through the ground floor, feeling the oppressive weight of Neos's proximity, tension rising in the silence, until Natalie said, "Whoa!"

Simon fired a reflexive burst of dispelling energy at the wall, and Lukas dropped into a combat stance as I shifted my grip on the dagger hilt. Then I saw what she was gaping at.

The tapestry with the sixteenth-century lady who looked just like me.

"Is that you?" she asked.

"My ancestor, I guess."

"The likeness is extraordinary," Simon mused.

"More like messed up," Natalie said.

"No wonder you're so emo all the time," Lukas said.

"Thanks." I stared up at it, trying to feel as powerful as that Emma looked. Had she ever faced someone as scary as Neos? Or been crushed by the voice of a siren? It didn't matter. They were here, and I was going to kill them, because that was the only way I could stop them. That was the messed-up part. Even though I didn't want to be like that Emma, I had no choice.

Natalie glanced at me, then at the tapestry. "Only one thing missing."

"What's that?"

"Her friends."

Lukas rolled his eyes, but I smiled at Natalie, and she grinned. She was true and loyal and somehow made searching a haunted mansion for a killer wraith master almost bearable. She'd protected me at school, and now it was my turn. I had to dispel anything that threatened her. And Simon and Lukas.

"Whenever you two are done with your Hallmark moment," Lukas said, "we might want to—"

My spine started tingling, and an instant later wraiths rose through the floor and attacked. The humanoid cockroaches swarmed toward us in a blast of frigid air. All my tension and fear dropped away as the hours of preparation kicked in. We were ready.

Instead of stepping away from the attack, Lukas lunged, using a wave of compelling force to crash into the wraiths, funneling them over his head to slam into the walls.

Simon's bursts of dispelling energy weren't much stronger than when I first met him—but he'd learned to aim them for maximum effect. He tore through a wraith in two seconds as summoning energy erupted from Natalie.

I dispelled the wraith trying to claw Lukas in the

back, and Coby and the ghost jocks materialized and demolished the last one.

And that was that. Just seconds after they'd attacked, we won. But it was too easy. There had to be more than this.

"Tell Coby and his team to scout the area," Simon told me. "We need to find Neos—and the siren." He swallowed. "And any survivors from the Knell."

You okay with scouting? I asked Coby.

No problem, he said, and led the jocks through a wall.

We swept the bottom floor, then went upstairs and checked the billiard room, the library, and a sitting room with views of a barren autumn garden. Then onto another set of stairs. Halfway up, I felt my anxiety ebb and I paused to smell a vase of roses on the landing.

We were going to win. This wasn't even hard. We didn't need to worry so much, or fight so hard. We didn't really need anything. This was all going to work out.

"Um, guys?" Natalie said, eyeing me.

She nattered a few words I couldn't quite make out above the humming in my head. And the guys got all concerned, for no reason in particular, with Simon inflating a bubble of dispelling magic and Lukas raking the walls with compelling force.

Then the siren appeared at the head of the stairs. She looked like that old silent-movie star with the bobbed hair, Louise somebody, except she wore a bright blue baby-doll dress, thigh-high black stockings, and faded black Converse All Stars.

Sweet Emma, my gemma, she said, her face shining with love and concern. *You don't need them. You don't need anyone*.

Simon loosed a burst of dispelling power that she didn't seem to notice, then Lukas blasted compelling magic at her, and she faltered.

But I need you, she continued. *I only want to talk and he's trying to kill me. Please! Please help me*.

"Stop that," I told Lukas.

Lukas grunted and doubled his attack, and the siren fell to her knees, weeping in pain. *Please, please*, she begged, as Lukas stepped closer.

"I said *stop*," I shouted, and slammed the heel of my hand into Lukas's chest.

He staggered backward and tumbled down the stairs to the landing, where he lay in a moaning heap.

"Emma!" Natalie grabbed my arm. "Look at me. She's in your mind, the siren's controlling you—"

I head-butted her, and she dropped where she stood, her forehead already red and swelling. Then I turned toward Simon, who ignored me, focusing all his meager power on the siren. His eyeglasses flashed and he muttered under his breath, while I spun into one of the unarmed stances that the Rake taught me.

Then I stopped, as the song in my head faded. Instead of focusing her power on controlling me, the siren was focused on fending off Simon's attack. I stood motionless, caught between her will and my own.

With the echoes of her lullaby ringing in my mind, I

couldn't fight her—but I knew what was happening now, and I kept myself from attacking Simon.

Instead, I stood there, completely useless. Rooting for him to beat her, but still unable to force the siren completely from my mind and help him.

Simon had never been powerful—and the siren shrugged off his blasts. I felt her lullaby grow louder and more persuasive as Simon uttered a few curses and threw everything into one last barrage. Her laughter was low and melodious, and she didn't give an inch.

Until Coby and the ghost jocks returned.

They flashed through a wall of portraits and I said, *Thank God! Stop her!*

But Coby said, *I'm sorry, Emma.*

And with gleeful grins, the ghost jocks slammed into Simon as Coby dove at me. Still under the siren's influence, I couldn't defend myself as he grabbed my arms and clamped them behind my back.

I felt the tingle of ghostburn, but he managed to use my sleeves to pin me without singeing my skin. He shoved me toward the second floor, and I heard Simon behind me, calling for help as the ghost jocks kicked him.

I stumbled forward, unable to comprehend what was happening. I couldn't reconcile my ideal of Coby—the guy I'd trusted completely—with what was happening. This wasn't Coby; he'd never betray me. This was something I'd dragged back from the Beyond that only *looked* like Coby.

"Coby, this isn't you." I halfheartedly struggled in his

grasp, unable to lift the siren's fog that curbed my abilities. "Please. Anyone else but you. You can't be the one who betrayed us."

Because if he was, I didn't know what I was fighting for anymore. I didn't want to kill Neos only to be with Bennett. I was here to avenge Coby's death.

I'm dead because of you, Emma, he said. *Did you really think I wouldn't blame you?*

I shook my head, but couldn't speak. He was right; it was my fault. All of it was my fault. His death, my family's disappearance, my team's defeat—my new family lying downstairs, battered and beaten, defenseless against Neos. And the Knell on the brink of extinction, its members being slaughtered one by one. Tears pooled in my eyes as I pictured Bennett the last time I'd seen him. If it weren't for me, he wouldn't be strung out on Asarum.

Did killing Neos even matter? The damage was already too great. Nothing I'd do would make anything better.

Coby dragged me through a labyrinth of hallways, and I lurched along defeated, the siren's lullaby ringing loudly in my ears. I welcomed her melody, the comfort and release. A moment later, Moorehead and Craven joined us, sneering about how they'd kicked Simon's ass.

Then Coby opened a door and pushed me into the study with the ornately carved fireplace. The same room where I'd killed my possessed aunt. The ghost jocks flanked me, and Coby and the siren followed, but I hardly noticed any of them.

Neos was waiting for me. *Darling*, he said, his voice scraping in my mind. *How I've missed you.*

The room was lit only by candlelight and the fire in the grate, and he sat in a wingback chair with two wraiths behind him, ectoplasmic drool dripping from their gaping mouths. Neos was in the same black shirt and pants he'd worn when he'd found me as a child. His eyes were jet-black and crowlike, and the sight of him made my teeth hurt.

Despite the siren's enforced calm, I felt a shiver of terror, and took a shuddering breath, panic beginning to overtake me. The siren's voice immediately sounded louder in my mind. *There's no need to fear. Let go of all your worries, all your responsibilities . . .*

Neos's bright eyes sought out Coby. *You served me well. You will be rewarded.*

The siren glided toward Neos and laid a hand on his arm, like a possessive girlfriend. *She is yours*, she told Neos.

At last. Neos eyed me hungrily. *Come here, girl.*

Coby shoved me forward, and I stopped a few feet from Neos. I didn't attack him, I didn't even think of attacking him. I stood with my head demurely bowed, the siren's endless song echoing in my mind.

Look at me, Neos said. *You're the key, Emma. My final rite.* He licked his fleshy lips. *I can almost taste you already.*

Thrumming beneath the siren's lullaby, like a dissonant chord, was the sense that everything had gone wrong. That I could change things. But knowing didn't help. I was powerless to do anything.

Then there was a flash of movement, as Coby dove away from me, shouting *Now!* at the ghost jocks.

He launched himself at the siren with the experience of a thousand tackles, and slammed into her brutally. Neos had kept his bodyguard wraiths in check, but with a brief wave of his hand, he released them. They flew to attack Coby—and the ghost jocks threw themselves into their path to block them.

My head felt cloudy, my thoughts drifting past half formed. I watched the jocks fending off the wraiths while Coby struggled with the siren, and nothing made sense.

Until, as Coby started choking the siren, she screamed at me to release her. *My Emma, help! Help me!* She grew stronger with fright. *Emma, they'll kill me. Please!*

My fury came in a rush, the siren thrusting all her fear and pain into my head. I felt the dispelling power like lightning in my veins. The light pooled inside my hands, growing brighter and stronger until I shot jagged bolts of energy at Coby.

He had betrayed me. Who did he think he was? I *made* him. I blasted him again as Neos cackled, discordant and bone-chilling.

The siren whispered to me, *He's nothing to you. Another meddler who plagues you with demands and problems—*

The ghost jocks deflected my blasts with their bodies, flickering as I chipped away at their spectral forms. Then Coby punched the siren hard in the stomach, and she released her hold on me. My mind began to clear.

Coby hadn't betrayed me. He'd pretended to side with Neos so they wouldn't see him as a threat—to get me close, close enough to kill Neos. It was brilliant. He'd played his role so well, I'd believed him. But I should've known he'd never betray me. He was Coby, and I could trust him to the very end. And the strength in that was enough to lift the siren's haze and propel me forward.

I drew my dagger and leaped at Neos, but he rose in a flash to the ceiling, crowing loudly. *The final rite is happening as we speak—and feeding me more power than you can imagine.*

He lifted his arms and summoned, and more wraiths swirled into the room in whirlwinds of filth and decay. They took form and started savaging Coby and the ghost jocks.

I flipped my dagger in my hand to throw at Neos, and three more wraiths rose in front of me. I kicked one in the throat and stabbed another in the gut and felt the chill fingers of the third clawing at my back.

I dropped and rolled and snapped its neck, but more formed even as the dead ones dissolved into greasy oil slicks on the Oriental carpet.

I heard Coby and the jocks losing their battle, and felt the siren clawing at my mind again—but she couldn't find a toehold. Maybe she couldn't slip into my head unless she preyed on my self-doubt, my fear. Right now, all I felt was anger.

Coby swore and Moorehead screamed, but before I could help, Neos flew at me.

I dodged, then spun to return the attack, but wraiths filled the room. I couldn't help Coby and the jocks—I couldn't even see them. I heard Moorehead scream again, and fought my way through the writhing mass of wraiths toward the sound. I stabbed two more wraiths before someone stepped through the door—shining with power and a rage that equaled my own. He wielded spears of light as easily as a couple of chopsticks.

Bennett.

Still wearing the faded-blue long-sleeve T-shirt and jeans. Still looking strung out. Still gorgeous enough to stop my heart, even now. He skewered four wraiths before they knew he was there. They hurtled at him, shrieking in hunger, and he burned them away into reeking wisps of smoke.

"Emma!" he shouted. "Finish him!"

His lance of light turned into a blade and sliced through the wraiths—and cleared an opening for me, to Neos.

I sprinted at Neos, jumping from a chair onto the desk, my dagger flashing as he fired spectral blades at me. I deflected them and fought closer and closer. As the battle raged behind us, Neos's power oozed at me from all around, oily black tentacles groping toward me, but I pressed forward, closer to those glittering black eyes.

Then Neos shouted a command, and a ghost dropped from the ceiling to hover between us. For a moment, I didn't recognize him; then I saw his big eyes and Dickensian outfit, and froze.

Nicholas! I said. *Are you all right? Did he hurt you?*

No, mum. He glanced fearfully at Neos. *Not yet.*

Sheathe the dagger, Neos sneered. *Or I will introduce your friend to places in the Beyond that can drive even a ghost mad.*

A wraith screamed behind me. I heard Coby grunt with effort, and Craven gasp. Dispelling lightning rods of power flashed. Yet all of that felt very far away—my whole world shrunk until nobody existed but me and Neos and Nicholas.

You'll pay for this, I said. *He's just a boy.*

Darling Emma, Neos said. *He's been a ghost for two hundred years. It is you who is the child. Sheathe the dagger. Oh, you* are *special, my little girl. I've never seen a ghostkeeper use a knife like that.*

Please, mum, Nicholas said, shaking with fright.

I lowered my dagger, my heart thundering in my chest.

"Emma!" Bennett yelled from behind me. "Whatever he's saying is a lie! Nicholas betrayed you—he's been spying for Neos."

I didn't turn my head; I didn't move an inch—but my mind worked furiously. I remembered the jolt of fear when Nicholas had approached with that icicle. I remembered him hovering in the hallways and at team meetings, always listening. And I remembered Nicholas had given me the metal disk that stank of Neos, and had lured us away from the museum. I looked at him and saw the truth in his eyes: Nicholas *was* working for Neos.

But we're family, I said to him.

My sister is my only family, Nicholas told me. *And Master Neos will bring her back*.

Master Neos is going to die, I said, feeling the force rumbling in my chest. *For the last time*.

Then I imbued my dagger with dispelling power and launched myself at Neos. I batted away his streams of perverted energy and slammed him into the wall. We fell to the floor and I slashed with my dagger—

And Nicholas flitted between us.

I pulled the blow at the last moment. I couldn't hurt Nicholas. After everything, I still couldn't hurt him.

Neos slammed me with a backhand that sent me reeling into a bookcase, and Nicholas streamed toward me, his face a mask of violence. A lance of Bennett's light flashed from behind me and hit Nicholas in the center of his narrow chest. He looked faintly surprised, and said, *Oh, mum . . .* Then he crumbled into gray ash and vanished.

"Nicholas!" I cried. "It isn't fair."

But there was no time to mourn as Neos roared.

He exploded with an avalanche of power that hurled me across the room, shredded his wraiths into nonbeing— and tore through Coby and Moorehead and Craven. They faded in an eyeblink, leaving the siren huddled on the floor, and even Bennett stumbled backward, his arms lowered after having dispelled Nicholas.

The final rite, Neos purred. *Nothing fancy. Nothing you haven't seen before. Taking power by sacrificing ghostkeepers.*

Well, I've got a stock of them in the basement—and three more just died to my wraiths. The Knell is gone, and I grow stronger with every sacrifice. And once I kill you—

I rose into a crouch, and the siren, unmoving in the corner, spoke into my mind: *Wait. Emma, wait.*

"Just him and us," Bennett said, wiping blood from his split lip, not realizing the siren was still conscious.

"Yes," I said.

Bennett killed Nicholas, the siren sung in my mind. *A little child. He likes dispelling too much—he's not a ghost-keeper, he's a murderer. He's on drugs, look at him. He's a killer of children.*

Bennett circled the room, fists crackling with energy, until we flanked Neos. "Whenever you're ready, Emma."

Whenever I was ready? For what?

I knew it. I knew I couldn't trust him. My parents were right. He'd left me when I needed him most, taken Asarum, and now he'd killed Nicholas, a member of my family. I was responsible for Nicholas, and Bennett had taken him away from me. He always had enjoyed dispelling too much.

I sprang at Bennett. He was so focused on Neos that he didn't see the blow coming. I kicked his feet from under him, and he hit the ground hard. I put my right boot on his wrist to keep him from dispelling.

My dagger felt heavy in my hand—heavy and strong and purposeful.

I knew how to use a knife. A strong blow didn't come from my wrist, but from my whole body. And now the blade slashed through the air toward Bennett's chest and I couldn't stop myself. He'd killed Nicholas, so I'd kill him.

The blade sliced downward, and I saw his face and remembered something he'd once said: *There are powers stronger than ghostkeeping.* I watched myself stabbing Bennett, and I saw his eyes widen with shock and fear . . . and love. Even as I killed him, the love shone undimmed in his eyes.

Neos crowed as my blade cut through Bennett's shirt and sliced his chest. But I never once stopped staring at his eyes. Those cobalt blue eyes that I dreamed of every night. Those eyes that I would never stop loving, no matter what Bennett did.

And an instant before the blade plunged into his heart, I pivoted and flicked my wrist. The dagger flung through the air and buried hilt-deep in the siren's throat.

She vanished instantly. I'd silenced her forever.

There are powers stronger than ghosts and ghostkeeping. There's love. And there's anger.

Bennett lay sprawled on his back with blood seeping from his wound, and I stood and faced Neos, unarmed. I'd always thought that anger felt hot. When I'd lose my temper, my face would flush—I'd want to scream as I boiled with rage, everything tinged with red.

Not this time. This fury was subzero. I didn't want to scream—I didn't even want to speak. Ice flowed through my veins.

They'd tried to make me kill Bennett. That was a mistake.

Across the ruined study, Neos grew denser and larger, still absorbing power as his wraiths sacrificed ghost-keepers in the basement. The air around him unraveled and formed a sword with a hungry keen edge, shining with blackness.

I stalked toward him bare-handed and he swung his sword. Shaped from shards of the Beyond itself, the blade could slice through life and death; I couldn't deflect it, not without my dagger.

I didn't need to. I was as powerful as Emma, the woman in the tapestry. I was as powerful as *me*. I stepped inside his swing—almost into his embrace—and for an endless instant we stood inches apart. His putrid breath touched my cheek, and power shimmered off him like heat off the sun.

I hooked my left hand under his elbow and drew him toward me, the last thing he expected. I imbued my right hand with dispelling power. Instead of imbuing my dagger, I imbued my flesh and blood that ran down through centuries, until my fist burned with a terrible white light.

Then I punched through the underside of his jaw. I wrapped my hand around the amulet embedded in his tongue and yanked.

Black blood spurted across the room and scorched through wood and cloth and leather. The howl as Neos faded into the Beyond was so full of agony and hate and power that it brought me to my knees.

Then silence. As everything evil faded away with him.

I shoved the amulet into my pocket and ran to Bennett. He'd been watching, his hands stanching the flow of blood. All I could see was the life left in his enormous blue eyes. He half smiled and said, "That was epic."

Then he passed out.

The team found me there later, cradling Bennett's head in my lap. Simon had called the Knell's doctor, and she'd already put Lukas's arm in a sling and tended the others' cuts and bruises. When the doctor saw Bennett, she shooed me away, muttering something about "Asarum," and began to disinfect and bandage the cut across his chest.

I told the team what happened, and Simon nodded grimly when I got to the part about Neos sacrificing the Knell ghostkeepers. He'd already found the basement with William's and Gabriel's bodies—and had refused to allow Natalie or Lukas inside.

"How are the ghosts?" I asked. "Coby and the boys?"

"They're in the Beyond," Natalie said. "I can feel them. Coby will be fine. You made him. The others . . . I don't know."

"What about Neos?" I said. "Coby betrayed him. Neos will go after him."

"Dude, what've you been doing?" Lukas said, his face paling. "Neos isn't dispelled?"

I shook my head. "He fled into the Beyond. He lost the amulet and the siren—and I guess most of his wraiths. But he . . . he's still strong. All those deaths."

"At least the siren's gone." Natalie rubbed her forehead. "I don't think I could take another head-butting."

I apologized and finished telling them what happened. Then Simon organized a search for survivors—both living and ghosts. I stayed behind, holding one of Bennett's purple-tinged hands.

When he finally stirred, he opened his eyes in panic and starting drawing on his powers, staring around the room with his fists clenched.

"Bennett," I said softly. "It's over."

When he realized I was there, the tension drained out of him. He smiled at me and said, "Hey there. I know you."

I buried my face in his neck. "I can't believe I stabbed you."

"Remind me never to get on your bad side," he said, and took my hand.

My hands didn't ache anymore, as if they'd been healed by all the dispelling energy, which took the pain and left faint white patterns etched into my skin.

"Are you coming back with us?" My voice filled with hope.

"Neos is gone," he said, with a slow, brilliant smile. "It's over. I wasn't kidding, Emma. Take my powers, take my past. All I want is you."

I swallowed. He didn't know. "About Neos . . ."

As I told him, the excitement and warmth in his face faded until nothing remained but a hard knot of purpose. "So he's not dispelled," he said. "And he massacred the Knell."

I closed my eyes against the pain on his face.

He traced a lock of my hair with his finger. "I need you," he said, "more than anything."

My eyes flashed open. "Then come home."

He showed me his purple hand. "Even with this? I can't stop, Emma. I still need to do what's right."

"Do you know what's right?" I leaned forward and kissed him. "This is right. You and me together."

"I know," he said.

I ran my hand down his chest and he gasped with pain. I pulled away and said, "I'm sorry!"

He smiled, a little sadly. "Me, too."

I blinked back my tears and didn't say anything else. I knew what he meant. We couldn't be together, not yet. Not until this finally ended, one way or the other.

21

Two weeks later, I still hadn't stopped crying. Every morning I'd wake and the tears would trail down my cheeks until a sob escaped. It took only one week before Natalie stopped knocking on my door, trying to comfort me. She finally understood there was no controlling the flow—those tears were the only thing that got me out of bed in the morning.

I sleepwalked through the final weeks of the semester, hoping that my grades in Latin and Trig would keep my GPA from disaster. I still wanted to go to college, after all—even if that seemed like an impossible dream, with the Knell failing and Neos still living in the Beyond.

On the last day of school before winter vacation, Sara invited me and Natalie to her house to celebrate. Lukas was standing with us at the gates, and Sara got a shy expression on her face before saying, "It's cool if you want to come, too. Though my surprise is for Emma."

"A surprise," I said, flatly. When Natalie poked me in the ribs, I added, "Can't wait."

"Wow," Sara said. "Get a grip on your enthusiasm, Emma."

I followed them to the car while Natalie explained about Bennett. I should've been mortified that my friends were discussing how devastated I was about a guy, but with Bennett it didn't matter. It was the truth and I didn't care who knew it.

We gossiped about school and vacation as we drove to the Neck. Sara's house was the perfect sea cottage, with views of the harbor and the village—if by cottage you meant five thousand square feet of polished wood floors, contemporary kitchen, and modern art. We grabbed sodas and chips in the kitchen, then headed upstairs to Sara's suite, where we found the surprise.

Harry sprawled over Sara's yellow satin sofa, looking like a boy with a great deal of experience in sprawling across sofas.

I smiled for the first time in weeks, and jumped into his lap. "I'm so happy to see you!"

"Then why are you crying?" he asked, wiping a tear from my cheek.

"Dude," Lukas said. "She does that now."

"What's wrong?" Harry asked. "Tell Uncle Harry everything."

"Bennett," Natalie explained.

"I knew you liked him," Harry said. "Ever since he tied your tie."

I started weeping again. "I hate you."

"Then why are you in my lap?" He grinned.

"Oh please," Natalie said. "As if you don't love having a pretty girl snuggle in your lap."

"Without paying for it," Sara added slyly.

"Ignore them." I stood and kissed him on the cheek. "I'm glad you're you again."

He turned serious for a moment. "Thank you, Emma. For everything."

Then Natalie popped her head into Sara's closet. "What can I borrow?"

"Anything," Sara said. "Oh, there's a leather jacket that'd be perfect for you. Now, where did I put that?"

Something rang false in her tone, and I eyed her curiously.

"Harry," Sara said, still stagy and forced. "Have you seen my leather jacket?"

He furrowed his brow. "I'll admit to keeping a close eye on your underthings, but your jacket? No."

"If only there was some way to find it," she said.

Then a short gray leather jacket with three-quarter sleeves floated into the room. Well, that's how it must've looked to Sara and Harry—but Lukas, Natalie, and I all saw Coby waving it back and forth in a ghostly fashion.

Coby! I said. *Where have you been?*

Here, mostly, he said with a grin. *After I reattached my limbs. Man, that Neos is nasty.*

You could've told me you were okay. I was worried.

He looked contrite. *Well, you wouldn't understand what*

it's like to need time to heal and mourn and cry. And cry, and cry, and cry . . .

I couldn't help myself. I laughed.

"What's he saying?" Sara asked.

So I told them. Apparently the three of them had been hanging out at Sara's house—almost like old times.

"Watch this." Harry pulled a beer can from beside the sofa.

"Harry!" Natalie scolded.

"It's empty. But watch. You know AA has twelve steps?"

He reached for the beer, and Coby snatched it away.

"He's like the thirteenth step!" Lukas said.

Harry beamed. "Exactly."

I spent the next couple of hours relaying messages back and forth, and felt better than I had in weeks. When Coby said he wanted to see me turn into a ghost again, I demurred, but he said I owed him.

Fine, I finally gave in. *But only because you're dead.*

That struck him as funny, and for the first time since I'd summoned him, I saw him laugh.

I excused myself to the bathroom, pulled Emma's ring from the chain around my neck, and slipped it on my finger. I slid through the door and flew up to sit beside Coby, where he was perched atop Sara's bookcase. I landed sort of awkwardly.

You need to practice that, he said.

I know, it's just so . . . weird.

You get used to it, Coby said resignedly.

I turned to look at him, still wearing the suit he'd worn for Homecoming, even more crazy good looking in death than in life. *Are you really okay? Even with Neos still out there?*

You kicked his bony ass, Em.

But he's still alive and you betrayed him. He'll come after you.

Probably. And he'll try to kill you, too. Coby took my hand, and he didn't burn me because we were both ghosts. *But you're a hero in the Beyond, Emma. Maybe he's not gone forever, but you beat him. Nobody thought that was possible. We were staring into the abyss, and you stopped him.*

I guess.

Stop guessing. He showed me one of his old charming grins. *Maybe you still gotta sweat the play-offs, but you know what? You won the game.*

We *won the game*, I said, and leaned against him.

Lukas glanced up at me, and I waved, but he ignored me, too interested in what Sara was saying. Though I noticed him glance at Natalie flirting with Harry, almost like he was jealous.

Which one is he into? Coby said. *Sara or Natalie?*

Sara, I think. I mean, he and Natalie . . . My voice trailed off. What if he and Natalie really were falling for each other? *Well, they're both ghostkeepers, so that'll never work. Anyway, Sara's still missing you, Coby. We all are.*

Yeah. But you know what? I think it's all going to be okay.

We sat there and watched our friends talking and laughing, and I started to think maybe he was right.

. . .

That night after dinner, I slunk into the kitchen and found
Celeste scrubbing pans and Anatole putting the finishing
touches on a homemade chai milk shake for me. I'd found
solace in the two of them lately, maybe because they were
the only ones who really understood how I felt about
Nicholas.

I'd failed him. I knew that he'd betrayed us, that he'd
almost killed us all. And I knew that Bennett did what
was necessary to protect me—to protect *everything*—but
I still missed the little urchin, with his big eyes and his
annoying *mum*s.

I helped Celeste dry the pots, then sat in the nook and
indulged in my milk shake. After a time, Celeste perched
on the bench across from me and did her sewing, then
Anatole huffed down beside me to engage in some menu
planning, which involved a surprising amount of gesticu-
lating and muttering.

After a while, I started feeling better. Sometimes just
sitting quietly was all I needed. I washed my milk-shake
glass and said good night to Anatole and Celeste. I'd hardly
said two words, but they knew I loved them.

Upstairs, I stepped into my room—then froze. A
strange shape sat on my bed. My powers flared before I
realized: "Bennett!"

His blue eyes were sunken and his black button-down
and tattered jeans hung on his sinewy frame, but his
smile was perfect. "Don't ask what I'm doing here."

So of course I said, "What are you doing here?"

"I couldn't waste another day."

"What does that mean?"

"You know what it means. Any day I don't spend with you is a day wasted."

My heart lifted. "Do the others know you're here?"

"No, I snuck in." He shot me a naughty grin. "I have a secret drainpipe."

He looked like hell, but all the charm and mystery I'd fallen in love with were still there. Just being in the same room with him made me feel more alive. "And what makes you think I'd collude with your sneakiness? There is an Englishman downstairs who'd like a word with you."

"The only one I want words with is you." He somehow made that sound sexy, and my body tingled—for once not because of ghosts. "I was wrong, Emma. We belong together."

"You don't think you'll . . ."

"Lose my powers?" He shrugged. "If I keep taking the Asarum, I'll be okay."

My stomach dropped. "Bennett, no. Please, stop. You're killing yourself."

"I can't stop." His eyes pleaded with me. "And I can't stay away from you."

I was quiet, not sure what to do. I couldn't stand what he was doing to himself, but the thought of him leaving made me shake.

"Then don't go." I pulled him close. He was right. We

had to be together. To love each other, no matter what the cost.

He smiled as he ran his hands over me in the moonlight and kissed me. As my eyes closed, I realized he was beginning to feel like someone else. Not the boy I'd spent a night with in New York. He smelled different, looked different, felt different.

And I wondered . . . could I love this Bennett just as much?

ACKNOWLEDGMENTS

Thanks to my agents, Nancy Coffey and Joanna Stampfel-Volpe, their assistant, Deirdre Sprague-Rice, and everyone at Bloomsbury, especially my fantastic editor, Caroline Abbey, and publicists, Deb Shapiro, Kate Lied, and Rachel Wasdyke. And thanks to Melissa Senate, who listens to every complaint along the way.

Lee Nichols was raised in Santa Barbara, California—the setting of her adult novels *Tales of a Drama Queen*, *Hand-Me-Down*, and *True Lies of a Drama Queen*. The first Haunting Emma novel, *Deception*, was her YA debut. She attended Hampshire College in Amherst, Massachusetts, where she studied history and psychology. She now lives in Maine and is married to novelist Joel Naftali.

www.leenicholsbooks.com

This ghostly mystery is not over yet.
Read on for a sneak peek at the next
Haunting Emma book:

SURRENDER

I've never liked bad boys. On TV shows, when the girl is torn between her sweet best guy friend—who is not-so-secretly in love with her—and the standoffish bad boy, I always root for the best friend.

But standing in Bennett's attic room, my arms twined around him, I finally saw the appeal. I shouldn't have been there. Shouldn't have let Bennett's drug-stained fingers stroke my neck, shouldn't have lied to Simon about him. And I definitely shouldn't have been kissing him when I was supposed to be downstairs with the rest of the team, trying to figure out Neos's next move.

Yet I barely protested when Bennett nibbled my neck. "I—I should—oh—"

He pinned me with his piercing blue eyes. "Yes?"

"Um . . ." I licked my lips. "I forgot what I was going to say."

"You don't have to say anything. Just keep making those little noises."

I let out a sound I didn't recognize as he traced my spine with his finger.

"Yeah, like that," he whispered.

Oh my God. How could I have been so wrong about bad boys? Forget the best friend, I wanted *this*—the unpredictable charm, the danger, and the heat. Did anything else matter? I closed my eyes and ran my fingers through his hair in the spinning darkness—then stopped when I heard a cough from the doorway.

My eyes snapped open and I caught a glimpse of someone standing at the top of the attic stairs. It was Simon, peering inside.

"Simon!" Bennett and I sprang apart. "Go away!"

"Emma . . . ," he said. And there was something weird in his tone, something more than just *I've caught you with your drug-addled boyfriend who shouldn't be living here.*

"What?" I asked. "What's happened?"

Before he answered, two people stepped into the room. Well-dressed, familiar, and completely unamused.

And Bennett said, "Mom . . . Dad?"

I've always had moments when I wished I could yell "Freeze!" and the world would stop, giving me a chance to think of a great comeback line, retake a test, or cancel the inane grin I just flashed the guy I was crushing on. This was the *queen* of all those moments.

What were they doing here? Well, yes, it was their house, but did they have to show up this very minute? Why not an hour from now when I'd be done with Bennett? Okay, I'd never be done with Bennett, but at least I might've been fully dressed. Instead I was wearing a lacy white tank top, which no parent would deem modest.

As I struggled to put on a sweater, my hand brushed against Emma's ring on its chain around my neck. I considered whipping it on and disappearing in a cloud of ghostly embarrassment. On the plus side, it would end this terrifying encounter; on the minus side, I'd be deserting Bennett, which seemed really cowardly. And maybe turning into a ghost wasn't the best way to impress his parents. I mean, as much as I could impress them, given the whole making-out-with-their-son thing.

"I want you to meet Emma," he told them, as though there were nothing awkward happening. "You've probably heard a lot about her."

"Hi," I squeaked.

"It's all true," he said, with an easy grin.

His parents didn't smile back. They just stood there, radiating disapproval, which gave me ample time to discover that Bennett got his looks from his mom, who was dark-haired and beautiful. She had on a long asymmetrical burgundy sweater over black fitted pants and low boots and wore her long hair slicked back in a ponytail. Carefully made up, her pursed lips caused the only apparent wrinkles. Bennett's eyes, though, came from his dad, who, aside from the blue marbles of brilliance under his furrowed brow, was almost completely gray, from his hair to his dress shirt and pants.

"The Sterns just got back from Europe," Simon said into the silence. "They arrived late last night."

Mr. Stern took a step toward Bennett. "What have you done to yourself?"

Mrs. Stern's gaze flicked from Bennett to me and back again. "This is worse than I thought. Much worse."

"So your flight was good?" Bennett said.

"You look like a"—his mother made a choking sound—"a ghost."

"A *junkie*," his father said.

"And these are my parents," Bennett told me. "John and Alexandra. They're very pleased to meet you."

Simon took pity on me. He motioned me toward him and said, "Emma, let's give the Sterns a few minutes alone."

Bennett squeezed my hand tightly before letting me go. I crossed the room and Simon slipped me a twenty and said, "Go into town and get yourself a chai."

I turned back toward Bennett, unsure whether I should leave him. But he wouldn't look at me. His body was rigid with anger and I decided I wasn't helping things by being there. I took the twenty and fled.

The walk back to the museum from the café was freezing, despite the half hour I spent warming up with the fire and the hot chai. Maybe I was just anticipating the inevitable cold front from Bennett's parents. I stomped through the pockets of ice on the museum drive, wondering why they had suddenly returned.

Because they knew Bennett was hooked on Asarum? Because I was living in their house? If they kicked me out, where would I go? Would Natalie come with me?

Inside, I shed my coat and went straight up to Bennett's attic room. "It's me," I called, climbing the steps.

He met me at the top and took my hand. "Are you all right?"

"I'm fine. I mean, I'm slightly embarrassed, but . . ." I stopped at the look in his eyes. "What? What happened?"

He dropped my hand and turned away, and I took in the state of the room. His drawers were ajar and a suitcase lay open on the bed. I recognized the pale blues and grays of his wardrobe, messily folded and stuffed in his bag.

"No," I said. "*No.* You can't go."

He sat on the edge of the bed. "C'mere."

I crossed the room and stood between his legs, looking down at him. I still felt a nervous shiver just being close to him, like the first time a guy you like kisses you. Maybe I'd never get over that feeling with Bennett.

He traced a finger down my arm. "It's hard to think when you're this close."

"Then stop thinking."

"We need to talk."

"No, we don't," I said, and kissed him. I just wanted to go back to before his parents interrupted us, before he'd started packing. I didn't care that we might get caught again, I needed to recapture the feeling that we could be together. That everything would be all right.

I kissed him and he pulled me onto the bed, shoving his suitcase to the floor, running his hands over my body. He made me feel beautiful, he made me feel like I was the only thing he ever dreamed about. But I couldn't stop thinking about that suitcase, and I pulled away.

"I'm going to miss that," he said.

"Then why are you leaving me again?"

"They kicked me out, Em."

"Your parents?"

A shadow of regret darkened his smile. "They told me to get off Asarum or leave."

"So get off it!" As beautiful as his smile was, it would've been so much better if he was off that herb that stained his fingers and killed his appetite. Plus, I wasn't convinced he ever slept anymore.

"I can't. Not yet. Not until Neos is dead."

I sat up on the bed. There was nothing to say about that; we'd already had the argument a dozen times. "How much do your parents hate me?"

His grin returned. "A lot."

"Then why are you smiling?"

"Because they're pissing me off. And I want them to be unhappy, at least for a while."

"Bennett, I don't want them to hate me."

He rolled over. "They don't know you, Emma. Once they do, they'll fall in love—like I did."

"But until then?"

He kissed me. "Just let me enjoy it."

We repacked his suitcase together. I never liked packing, but folding Bennett's worn shirts and fraying khakis felt intimate, meaningful. I promised myself I'd never start wearing an apron with heels and packing his lunch, but I wanted to help—to stay with him as long as I could.

"Where are you going?" I asked. "Back to your dorm?" I could live with that. His room at Harvard was only forty minutes away.

"No, I'm still on leave. You know they want Simon in charge of the Knell? Well, he asked me to go along, to protect him."

"God knows he needs protecting." Simon's powers had never been strong, but what he lacked in strength, he made up for in knowledge. I couldn't help thinking that Simon might persuade Bennett to kick the Asarum while they were both at the Knell—in fact, I wondered if that wasn't part of his plan. I knew better than to mention it, though. "Who put Simon in charge?"

"The few ghostkeepers who survived Neos's massacre."

I paused, midfold. "How were all those deaths explained? Neos's wraiths must have killed twenty people."

"There are ghostkeepers everywhere, Emma. The Knell's been sending low-powered ghostkeepers into police departments and the FBI for generations. The official report says that a gas line exploded."

"They've got an answer for everything," I said bitterly. "Maybe they should've come up with a way to stop Neos before any of this happened."

I was devastated by the deaths of my aunt Rachel and all those other ghostkeepers, but I still wasn't ready to forgive the way the Knell had treated me or my family. And it made me sick sometimes, how everyone who worked for them was so devoted. Including Bennett and Simon.

Bennett tossed a pair of socks into his suitcase and watched me silently. He'd grown up with the Knell; he'd always be loyal to them. It was an old argument he clearly didn't want to reopen.

"It doesn't matter," I said. "Everything will change with Simon in charge. He deserves your protection. I'm glad it's you."

I tucked the last T-shirt into his suitcase, and he flipped the lid closed, then rested one drug-stained hand on the back of my neck. "I don't want to leave you," he said.

I kissed his gaunt, beautiful face, not liking that I was getting used to the way his looks and scent had changed since he started taking Asarum. "I know," I said. "But it's not forever."

"No," he said, "it's not forever."

And I repeated it to myself: he wouldn't have to be

like this forever. But with Simon's warnings about Asarum ringing in my head, I just hoped I was right.

Simon was waiting downstairs, his suitcase packed. He was dressed in the camel hair coat he'd first shown up in, and the sight of it made my heart break. I hadn't known him long, but he'd been an amazing guardian. Like the nerdy but cool, young uncle you always wished you had. I couldn't believe I was losing him along with Bennett. I threw myself at his chest, hugging him hard.

"I'm going to miss you so much. And I don't think I've ever said thank you."

"Bloody hell, Emma." He grinned at me. "Stop before you make me cry."

Natalie stormed into the foyer. "Bloody hell is right. What the fu—"

"Natalie!" I said, cutting her off. Not that I minded her swearing, but I knew the Sterns were around and didn't want them thinking any worse of us.

She strode to the front door and leaned against it, crossing her arms. "You can't go. Neither of you. I won't let you."

"Natalie—" Bennett started.

"We're a team," she interrupted. "We need to stay together. You're letting them break us up."

"I *am* them now," Simon said. "I'm only doing—"

"Emma needs you both," she said. "You know Neos is

coming back, and every time he comes back, he comes back stronger. I can't protect her—I can't even protect myself!—and I'll be damned if she gets hurt because she's worried about me, so no, you're not leaving. You're not going anywhere."

"Come here, my little Fury," Simon said.

Natalie crossed the hall to him, a stubborn glint in her eyes, and he spoke quietly to her. I wanted to go comfort her, but Bennett stopped me. "Let them talk."

"She *is* kind of like one of the Furies," I said; I knew from Latin classes they were goddesses of revenge.

"If anyone's a Fury, it's you," Bennett murmured back.

Before I could respond, I noticed the Sterns in the hallway that led to Mr. Stern's office. They stood disapprovingly, eyeing the scene Natalie was making. She was taking this harder than I expected, and I wished Lukas was here to make a joke and ease the tension. After Simon comforted Natalie for another minute, Mrs. Stern cleared her throat.

Simon winced. "Ah, yes. One more thing."

"They're kicking us out?" Natalie hiccupped.

"No, no," Simon said. "Quite the opposite. The Sterns have agreed to act as your guardians."

I glanced at them, thinking Simon should've added the word *reluctantly* somewhere in that sentence.

Natalie snorted. "Another day, another guardian."

"I know." Simon laid a hand on her shoulder. "You get tossed around a lot. And if it were anyone else, I'd worry. But you two will be okay."

Natalie sniffled some more, then pecked Simon on the cheek and crossed the room to fiercely hug Bennett. She gave the Sterns one last evil look, then ran upstairs in a burst of tears. Yikes. Not her most shining moment.

"Well, she's a bit high-strung," Mr. Stern said, and I was surprised at how deep and warm his voice was.

"How about this, Dad?" Bennett said. "You hold off judging Natalie until after you battle Neos a couple times, then we'll see who's high-strung. She doesn't have half of Emma's power—hell, she's a *summoner*—and she's faced down a vicious nightmare without flinching. You have no idea what we've been dealing with."

"Bennett," his mother said warningly.

"When Neos killed Olivia," Bennett asked his father, "what did you do?"

"Bennett!" his mother snapped.

"I mourned," his father said.

"Well, right, yes," Simon blurted. "We should be on our way. I'm sure Natalie will be just fine. She's got Emma to look after her."

"But who's going to look after Emma?" Bennett asked.

I leaned into him, standing as close as I could without actually touching him. I hated that we had an audience for our final moments together. Especially when that audience was his parents and Simon. "Just come back to me safe," I answered. "That's how you can take care of me."

"I promise," he said. Then he kissed me, a full-on everything-you've-got kiss, like he didn't care that his parents were standing twelve feet away from us. And at that moment, neither did I.

That night, I stood at my bedroom window, hoping I'd see Bennett's Land Rover pull into the drive, knowing I wouldn't. I waited anyway, thinking maybe Coby would come strolling through the maples. But he'd been spending more time with Harry and Sara now that they knew he was a ghost. They couldn't see or talk to him, but the three of them found ways to communicate.

I wanted someone to distract me, to help me forget about missing Bennett, and for a moment, I thought the figure drifting through the trees was Coby, granting my wish. I opened my window, a half-smile on my face—then realized it wasn't him. It was another ghost, a woman wearing a long white nightgown. I didn't know who she was, but for some reason the sight of her wandering through the trees reminded me of mad Ophelia in Shakespeare's *Hamlet*. Like when she got closer, I'd see flowers woven through her hair and a crazy look in her eyes.

Except as she shifted from the darkness of the maples into the moonlight, I recognized her. "Rachel?"

I thought I saw her smile faintly before she turned, her attention suddenly on the distant tower of Thatcher, peeking over the museum's walls.

Aunt Rachel, I said, sputtering in surprise. *What . . . what are you—how are you—*

She didn't answer. She drifted in the direction of